Zoey Lee
Schoolyard Scuffle

This book belongs to:
_____

for **Bodhi**, who carved a new path through the jungle,

for **Meijin**, who filled it with light,

and for **Pawan**, who walks it with me.

ZOEY LEE: Schoolyard Scuffle

Text and Illustrations copyright © 2011 by Lisa M. Ling

All rights reserved.
No part of this book may be used, reproduced or transmitted in any manner whatsoever without written permission from the publisher except in the case of brief quotations embodied in critical articles and review.
For information address:
FEAR2LOVE Press, PO Box 1824, Point Roberts, WA, 98281.
info@fear2lovepress.com

This is a work of fiction. Names, characters, places, and incidents either are the product of the author's imagination or are used fictitiously. Any resemblance to actual persons, living or dead, events, or locales is entirely coincidental.

Illustrations by Fred Sherman

Published by FEAR2LOVE Press.

ISBN-13: 978-1-937861-00-1
ISBN-10: 1937861007

Library of Congress Control Number: 2011942293

1

Welcome to My World

"Zoey, wake up!" her mom called from downstairs. "You're going to be late!"

Zoey's eyes slid open slowly despite the urgency in her mom's voice. She glanced over at her clock and knew she still had time. As she rolled over in her cozy, goose-down comforter, she closed her eyes again. *Just a few more minutes of sleep,* she thought. *It's only 7.30...*

"ZOEY LEE! WAKE UP!" Her mom shouted again, a few minutes later.

"Okay, okay, I'm coming," Zoey replied lazily, still half asleep. She knew she'd face her mom's wrath if she didn't get moving soon. She sat up in bed, rubbed her eyes, yawned and stretched her arms. Looking out her frosted window, she could see the tall evergreen trees in their backyard still white-tipped with snow. They seemed to go on forever in the distance, bordered only by imposing mountains, with no other houses in sight. The view was very familiar — she'd spent her whole life in this place.

When's it gonna warm up? she wondered. *We do get spring, even way up north in this tiny little town. Winter should be almost over coz today's the last day of March...*

Bleary-eyed, she stumbled to the bathroom, dabbed her wet toothbrush and started brushing. As she looked at herself in the mirror, mouth full of minty foam, she couldn't help notice her big buck teeth.

"Gawd, I hate these beaver teeth," Zoey said to herself with disgust.

She always got broccoli stuck in them and ended up walking around with little green bits poking out her mouth...

Why'd I have to have such big front chompers that stick out so much? she asked the mirror. *Maybe braces'll fix that. But, OUCH! Very painful. Abby's always complaining about how much her braces hurt, especially when she goes to the orthodontist to get them tightened. She can barely even touch her teeth together, let alone eat anything crunchy for a whole week after her appointments. If I had braces, eating apples (which I love), would be totally out of the question... every bite would be like an explosion of pain ripping through my mouth...*

Zoey washed little chunks of sleep out of her brown eyes and combed her long hair, including the orange chunk that flashed boldly from her bangs. It was a reminder of a science experiment gone bad. She and

Abby were supposed to condense a special acid with a bunsen burner, but the glass beaker exploded instead, spraying chemicals in Zoey's face. Luckily, with her well-trained, cat-like reflexes, she managed to protect her face with her hands, but her hair wasn't so lucky. Most of it was tied back and therefore spared, but the bit at the front, her bangs, got seared. First they turned bright red, then gradually purple, blue, green and yellow depending on which shampoo she used. With grapefruit shampoo, her hair finally settled on orange. Without knowing it, she'd made the color permanent. The chemical in her hair had reacted with the citrus in the shampoo to burn each hair right down to the root. Now she kinda took it as a badge of honor — a freak accident that made her look that much more unique. She figured it had better grow on her since it wasn't growing out.

She continued to scan her facial features and olive complexion. *Nice nose,* she said to herself. *Fine, yet sturdy and evenly balanced from one nostril to the other. Quite a fine specimen, if I do say so myself...* She took a deep breath, then exhaled as hard as she could. *Man, can those babies flare out!*

Then she scowled, noticing the red splotches scattered across her face. *You could do with a few less zits, girl. Maybe, uh... wash your face a bit more?!*

Zoey's inner dialogue was already going strong first thing in the morning and it wasn't all that pleasant. She moved in for a closer look and saw a few zits on her forehead, still too small to do anything with. *Ahh, but here's a good one. A nice 'ripey' on my cheek. I know this isn't a good idea, but I'm gonna do it anyway... I'm gonna squeeze this baby like a cream puff...* She pressed two fingers down hard on her face, just below her cheekbone. Whitish puss oozed out, leaving a nice red blotch outside her hairline. She frowned, suddenly disgusted with herself.

Great, that mark's wildly unflattering, kinda like my front teeth. Geez, I just had to do that, didn't I? Don't you ever learn, Zoey? Don't squeeze 'em, tweeze 'em...

"Zoey, get down here and eat breakfast — NOW!," her mom called. "It's already 7.45. Mrs. Hornby, the bus driver, won't wait for you if you're late, you know. And I have to go to the office so I can't drive you."

Zoey quickly changed into her favorite lime-green t-shirt and torn blue jeans — her clothes were somewhat of a point of contention between her and her mom.

Why can't I wear an orange t-shirt with red shorts to school? Who cares anyhow? If it fits and it's comfy, what gives?! But NOOO... mom says my outfit should match... at least a little. Orange and red don't go together. Orange and green don't go together. In fact, orange doesn't go with much — but it happens to be my favorite color! I've got about five orange T's, an orange backpack, orange sneakers, even an orange cell phone case... Oh and an orange baseball cap from the leftover dye we used for my orange belt. What an ordeal that was... supposed to be easy — just heat the water, drop in 1 teaspoon of orange dye and boil the belt for three minutes. We did that, but when we pulled it out, it was a funny brownish color. Kind of a cross between puke yellow and rust. Not at all the brilliant orange I had imagined. I guess the part we forgot was that my belt was yellow to start with, not white like it said on the package — oops...

The Lee house was large. All five bedrooms were upstairs, one for each of the four Lee kids and of course her parents room. From the stairway you could look down into the kitchen, dining and living rooms because of the vaulted ceiling. At the bottom of the stairs, on the main level was the front entrance. A hallway to the left led to the laundry room (with a laundry chute running between the two floors), bathroom, her parent's den and TV room. Another flight of stairs led down to the basement, which housed the dojo (martial arts training gym), wood stove, storage room and Zoey's favorite — the ping pong table.

Zoey ran downstairs, spinning around the square pillar on the landing, jumping three full steps onto the hardwood floor as she reached the main level of the house.

"Do you *have* to do that, Zoey?" her mom asked in exasperation.

"Do what?!"

"Jump down the stairs like that! You know I don't like it."

"You don't like a lotta things," Zoey mumbled under her breath.

"There's a bunch of cereal boxes in the cupboard. Take your pick. Milk's in the fridge — I gotta run sweetie. Got a big meeting this morning with a partner from another firm. Have a nice day. See ya later." Her mom grabbed her purse and keys and headed for the door.

"Oh yeah and tell your dad that I'll be late tonight. I'm preparing plans for the new building down at the marina. We've got to have them ready by tomorrow or the building permit will be revoked."

"Yeah, sure mom, no problem..." Zoey's head was still buried in the cereal cupboard. She heard the clickety-clack of her mom's heels on the wood floor, then the front door slam shut.

As if it makes a difference what I think anyway. Nice way to wake up... You shout at me, then tell me what not to do and rush out the door as soon as I see you. Oh and then you tell me to have a nice day? Have a nice LIFE, eh?

Just then Zoey's mom burst in the door again. "I forgot — gotta talk to your dad about something..."

Eating her cereal, staring absently out the window, Zoey heard loud voices coming from the study. Her dad had been working since early in the morning, preparing for

a prosecution at the local courthouse. She knew not to disturb him when he was in his den with the door closed.

"Don't tell me what to do, woman!" she heard her dad raise his voice.

"I'm not, I just want to make sure she gets her music practice in too," her mom replied.

"Well, training is just as important as piano. The girl's got plenty of time in the morning to practice." The irritation in her dad's voice was rising...

"She can't just kick and punch every morning. We're paying a pretty penny for her music lessons and she hasn't been practicing. She needs to spend time at the piano and mornings are the only time I have to make sure she does it," her mom continued, straining to remain calm.

"I have a solution," Zoey interjected quietly. She stood at the edge of the room, unable to contain herself any longer.

"What is it?" both parents asked in unison, turning to look at her.

"I'll quit both," she said softly. Her eyes welled with tears and she left the room.

Her mom followed her down the hall, into the kitchen.

"Zoey, honey, don't worry — we'll find a better solution. I know you don't want to quit your lessons... I know you love that stuff... But let's talk about it tomorrow. Your dad's busy preparing for the Corvatch trial — you know the guy who stole thousands of dollars from the smelter — and I really gotta run now. See ya sweetie." She gave Zoey a kiss on the forehead and rushed out the door.

Zoey watched her mom disappear out the large cedar double doors. Her head reeled with thoughts. *That's not why I'm crying mom. I just want a little attention from you. Is that so much to ask? You're so busy with your big important projects and making money, that you've forgotten about me! Being the third kid out of four has it's advantages sometimes — like how my two older sisters have already broken all the rules, so I don't have to. But sometimes I feel invisible — like I could just drop off the face of the earth and no one in this family would even notice... And oh, by the way, I hate it when you and dad fight...*

Out of the corner of her eye, Zoey spotted her little brother with his coat and backpack on, opening the front door. Her sisters had already left on an earlier bus that took them to the high school.

"Darn! I'm gonna miss the bus!" Zoey said, snapping out of her self-pity. She pulled on her grey winter coat, grabbed her backpack and rushed down the long asphalt driveway after him just as the school bus rumbled up towards 37 Rainbow Road. She glanced up at the green and white street sign near the driveway. Their house was the only one on that side of the street, with a large semi-circular driveway that seemed to stretch on forever, especially when it came time to shovel it in winter. *Hmmph.*

Rainbow Road. Cudda picked a better name for our street, she thought. *Not so sun-shiney here. Oh, I forgot, it's named after a fish, not a sky-full of beautiful colored light. Yeah, that makes more sense...*

Pressing her face against the bus window, she watched their green and white house disappear around the corner, then settled in for the ride to school. Zoey and her family lived in a subdivision called Cablecar, about 5 miles out of town, where the land lots were bigger and you could keep animals. *As if this little town weren't remote enough... we have to go and live way outside it!*

Fifteen minutes later, the bus came to a stop at a small school with a flag pole out front. A blue snowflake on a white background fluttered in the wind — the Mattiki municipal flag. A single, one-story, peach colored building stretched across an expanse of greenish-brown grass. A chipped concrete path led from the bus-stop to the front door of the school. Another path led around the school to the playground, sports field and parking lot behind it. The school sat on a slope, so although it looked like a one-story building from the front, it was actually two stories high at the back. A large rectangular block stuck out from back of the school — the gym, with a ceiling high enough to play volleyball in. Bordering the school on the far side of the sports field was a paved road, one of the main drags that wound around the small town.

Zoey glanced at the sign on the front lawn and noticed for the first time how the words "Eagle Elementary School" matched the peach color of the building. *Yuck! I can't stand that color. Why couldn't they have painted the school orange, or blue, or something... anything else but peach. Thank goodness we don't have to wear uniforms — I don't think I could handle dressing in peach every day...*

A familiar voice greeted her as she climbed off the bus. "Hey, good morning Zoey".

"Hi Abby, how ya doin'?" The two friends walked together toward the sports field at the back of the school.

Abby looked distinctly cheery in her hot pink shirt with frilly edges and a heart shaped necklace. She wore a black skirt with it to hide her chubby butt. Her fingernails were painted purple with a matching purple hair band holding her short strawberry blond hair off her round face. She was shorter and stubbier than Zoey, but didn't seem to care in the least.

Although she and Zoey couldn't have looked more different, they had been best friends since third grade. They were inseparable. Both had felt like fish out of water at Eagle Elementary, not fitting into any of the standard cliques — jock, nerd, preppy, rocker, or bum. But since they found each other, they felt a lot more relaxed at school, happily doing their own thing, not caring what anyone else thought of them. Abby knew Zoey all too well and Zoey trusted Abby completely.

"What's up? Why the sour face?" Abby asked.

"Oh, yunno, just stuff..." Zoey lowered her eyes.

"Whaddya mean — 'just stuff'. What's goin' on Zoey?" Abby stared at her best friend with genuine concern.

They walked in silence for a few steps. "What's the matter, cat got your tongue?"

Zoey didn't feel like talking, but realized Abby wasn't gonna let it rest. *Isn't that what BFF's do? Pick you up when you're down?* She paused, then looked up at her friend in bemused exasperation..."Oh, alright then — I'll tell you!"

"I can't stand it when my parents fight. They act like I'm not listening, but I hear *everything*. Makes me feel awful — like a big rock landed in the pit of my stomach and a dark cloud's hanging over me that just won't go away." Now that the floodgate was open, Zoey's emotions poured out.

"They give us tons of *stuff*... but I don't want stuff. I want to do stuff with them. And not when they're talkin' on their cell phones or tappin' their blackberries. I want *time* when they're just paying attention to me and that's it. 100% ME TIME. Does that sound selfish? We could be doing anything — it doesn't really matter what. I don't even care. I just wanna feel their love. Is that too much to ask? I mean, I am their daughter after all. But they're too busy...always too busy."

"Wow, I didn't know you felt that way," Abby swung her arm around Zoey's shoulder.

"You're so lucky Abby. *Your* parents don't fight."

"Yeah, right! That's what *you* think. They just don't fight in *front* of us. There's a big difference. We still feel it when they're mad at each other. You can cut the tension in the house with a knife, even if nasty words aren't flyin' back and forth."

"Well, whenever I come over, it's always so peaceful and your mom's home — with home-made cookies in the cupboard! How awesome is that?! I wish my house were like that...," Zoey said wistfully.

"You think it's cool to have your Mom home all the time?" Abby raised her eyebrows in surprise. "Means she knows everything you're doin'. Sometimes I'd like to be a little more anonymous — know what I mean...? I have to admit though, I do like the whole freshly baked cookie thing after school — chocolate chip's my favorite, but mom also makes apple tarts, cinnamon buns —"

"STOP! Enough already! You don't have to rub it in!" Zoey laughed. "I'm already jealous that you can get home ten minutes after school's out to eat your goodies when I have to wait for the stupid bus..."

RRRRINGGGG — the first bell of the day sounded. Students poured into the hallway of the school from outside. The quiet corridors erupted with the noise of chattering friends, scuffling feet, backpacks unzipping, kids laughing and calling out to each other.

Zoey turned to her buddy. "Thanks for listening Abby. I feel a whole lot better."

"No prob Zoey. That's what friends are for."

2

Get Ready to be Creamed!

"Hey, watch out!" Zoey cried, as her armload of books dropped to the floor, cascading down the grey cement staircase. A rush of adrenaline surged through her veins as she stumbled to collect herself. Stooping down to pick up her blue and white striped pencil case, she expected to hear an apology from whoever did this. Instead, only laughter rang through the main stairway of Eagle Elementary. As she spun around in the direction of the sound mocking her, the lock of orange hair at her forehead came untucked from beneath her hairpin, flashing a bit of fire that matched her rising temper.

"Should've known it was you," she scowled in a deepish voice at the boy standing a few feet away. He watched her as she tossed her ponytail of dark hair behind her bony shoulders. His wavy blond hair swished carelessly around

his face, a long-sleeve light blue surfer t-shirt and baggy dark green cargo pants covered his lanky frame.

"You should watch where you're going, Zoey," he quipped, a look of superior disgust written all over his face. Although he knew their crash was entirely his fault, he felt he could say whatever he wanted to her and she wouldn't be able to do a thing.

He turned to his two friends standing beside him and snickered under his breath, "hmmph...what's this quiet, nerdy-smart girl gonna do anyway? She doesn't even have any friends."

"What?! Watch where *I'm* going?!" Zoey's eyes grew wide behind her golden glasses. "You're so rude. You could just say sorry you know."

"Why say sorry to an *IDIOT*? You're the one with *slitty* eyes that can't really see anyway." He had emphasized those two words on purpose, then stared her down and scanned for her reaction.

Zoey felt anger rise in her small, lean 4'10" body, like a volcano about to erupt. She stood in the middle of the school stairway, wearing a lime green t-shirt and slightly torn jeans. The orange sneakers on her calloused feet matched the lock of hair at her forehead. The deep heat spread upward, as if it could melt the glasses off her face. With her orange hair flashing, she wanted to *SCREAM* at him!

This wasn't the first time he'd done something like this. Zoey had seen him bullying other kids before. He was in her bad books before this thing even started.

The boy turned a cold shoulder at Zoey, moving away to talk to his friends. Shocked by this additional scorn, Zoey was about to lunge at him right there and then, but...

Suddenly, she felt a hand on her shoulder. Glancing to her left, she saw who it was and knew exactly what that touch meant... *calm down girlfriend, just calm down. Don't Xplode! here in the middle of school or you'll go to the principal's office. And no one wants that...*

"Uh, Zoey, you do know who that is, don't you...?!" Abby whispered frantically in her friend's ear, her hand still resting on Zoey's shoulder.

"Yes, I know who that is," Zoey whispered back, "and I'm not afraid... uh... well... maybe just a little..."

"Let's get outta here and get to class — *pronto!*," Abby said. "Come on, I'll help you pick up your stuff..."

"Hold on a sec —" Zoey turned to look her friend in the eye, testing to see how serious she was. "It's not like he's the Lochness Monster or anything — he's just a guy."

"Uh...yeah — just the captain of the basketball and swim teams. Like, the most popular guy in the entire school... or have you forgotten?" Abby asked with a hint of sarcasm.

"Like I said, he's just a kid, like me and you, not a monster. It's not like he has special powers or anything," Zoey said firmly.

"No," Abby agreed, "he can just swim circles around everyone in the school, throw hoops better than anyone else and run faster than a mad dog!" Abby scrunched her face and raised her flabby arms to make her point. Zoey could see a ring of sweat under her pits and realized Abby must be really stressed out to be secreting that much juice on what was not exactly a hot day...

"Oh yeah, well maybe he does have something in common with the Lochness Monster after all — that whole fish in the water thing..." Zoey smirked to herself.

"Look, let's just forget this and get outta here before this goes bad." Abby was getting a little desperate now.

Maybe I should take off and just leave this whole scene behind, Zoey thought for a split second as she felt the intensity of Abby's fear and watched the tall boy laugh easily with his friends. He seemed totally oblivious to the hushed conversation that was going on between the two girls, as if they didn't even exist.

He thinks he's so cool... cool enough to ridicule other kids. And when he does, they just walk away. So it's not like he's gonna stop doin' it anytime soon... It's not fair. No one stands up to this guy. No one makes him stop! Hmmph. Well, we'll see about that.

Zoey's thoughts gained momentum and power as they flowed through her mind.

Just then Zoey felt her glasses slide down her sweaty nose. Little smudges of steam formed on the lenses from the intense heat that seeped out of her body. She became abruptly aware of the scream lodged in her throat and the raised hair at the back of her neck. Pulling away from Abby's hand on her shoulder, she considered decking the guy right there, but remembered what happened to Ben Richfield when he punched out Sammy Sontmeir for calling him a fat pig. Ben had to go to the principal's office and write 200 lines of "I will not punch other kids at school, no matter what they call me."

How unfair! she thought, *Ben was just defending himself and he gets punished. Nawh, I'm not gonna punch you out right here and get nailed for it dude, I'm smarter than that. But don't worry, you'll get what you deserve...*

"If you're gonna call me names, you'd better be able to back it up," Zoey shouted out. Her orange bangs flared wildly across her forehead now.

As soon as the words were out, doubt set in. *What was that? 'If you're gonna call me names, you'd better be able to back it up???' I feel like my body and mind were just in a tug-o-war and my body won out...*

"Why? Whatchu gonna do about it — HUH?" the boy taunted back as he glanced confidently at his friend standing beside him, absolutely sure Zoey was bluffing.

OHMAGOSH, I'm trapped. Why'd I have to go and say that? Yeah, you're mad girl, but do ya have to make it worse? Could you've just kept your big mouth shut for once? Her mind searched for a way out, but Zoey realized there was nowhere else to go.

With a deep breath, she clenched her fists by her side in a grip that was very familiar to her. She spoke slowly, with all the calm she could muster... "Let's see whatchu got Kev. Meet me behind the parking lot — tomorrow, after school." As she heard the words of challenge spill out of her own mouth, a steely resolve washed over her. *I've never been in a fight at school before, but this one's unavoidable. I can't let him get away with it this time. I'll show him not to call me names...*

"Hah, you think I'm gonna fight a girl?!" Kev scoffed as he started to walk away, his blue eyes glistening with surprise. After a few steps, he stopped, then slowly turned to face her again, a sly smile creeping across his face. "Well, I suppose you're not just any girl with all that training you do... Okay, you're on Zoey. I'll be there. *Get ready to be creamed!*"

3

A Filly is Born

Zoey slammed her hand down on the alarm clock to shut off the annoying beeping.

Hmmph. Chores, before school. Who else has to do that? she whined to herself. *What's with parents and this whole 'work before play' thing anyway? Don't they know that if we enjoy something, we'll do it? And if we don't like it, a herd of wild elephants couldn't get us to do it — not regularly, not with a smile on our face and certainly not without pestering us until they go hoarse, that is. They think they're here to teach us all the stuff we need to know about life. Don't they realize we can teach them a thing or two too? Like laughing more?! Having more fun?! Letting loose?! Enjoying the moment?! Being totally consumed by — NOW?!*

She lay there, staring up at the white stucco ceiling, thinking of how the little bits of plaster might feel against her bare feet. Rough. Ouch. Too bad my legs aren't long enough to reach up there... oh, but they feel long when I do a nice good front kick... slowly, her mind drifted to what had happened the day before...

Don't they get that their words have way less impact on us than their feelings? We can totally feel their energy — like if they're in a crap mood, worried about something, or scared, you think we don't sense it? Yeah, right — it's as obvious as elephant poop is to a dung beetle, or the smell of melted chocolate is to me. Anyway, chores before school isn't even 'work before play', it's 'work before more work'. Speaking of which, I feel like crap this morning. Could it have something to do with how lousy my day was yesterday... my parents fighting before school, then Kev calls me names and I pick a fight with him... ya think?!

Zoey dragged her butt out of bed and hauled it downstairs, tiptoeing quietly. *That's the last thing I need,* she thought, *a pesky little brother following me around, or mom telling me what to do. I just wanna be alone for awhile.* She slipped out the side door of the house before anyone could hear her.

Makeshift wooden steps led down from the side door into a small covered area which separated the house from a double garage. A row of gum-boots of varying sizes lay next to the steps, with a selection of shovels, rakes and other yard tools hanging on the wall. A home-made doghouse and a snowblower filled the rest of the space.

Behind the house lay a huge backyard, bordered only

by pine trees and a deep lagoon beyond, strictly off limits because there were wolves and bears down there — at least that's what her mom said. Zoey had never seen a wolf in the wild before, but she'd seen plenty of bears. They came into their backyard during the summer, out of curiosity, or to steal food that was lying around. Her family had to be careful to keep all their trash stowed tightly in garbage cans and make sure the dog was with them when they were out back. Bears didn't come into their yard all the time, but often enough to make you think about it. It seemed that every year there was a story about a kid or dog who'd been mauled by a bear in the gulley near Zoey's school. She never actually knew anyone who'd been attacked, but with nine thousand people in the town, it was big enough for that to be not too surprising. However, she believed the stories and stayed away from the gulley and the lagoon.

A deep inhale of the cool, crisp northern air snapped her out of her self-imposed, one person pity party. *Girl, whatchu talkin about — feelin' like crap? You loooooove being outside...*

Zoey purposely left her black and red checkered wool jacket unbuttoned, despite the chilly morning air. She liked the feeling of goosebumps on her skin and shivers down her spine. *Ymmmm, cool... makes me feel A-Live — like all my senses are working even though my mind's still a groggy mess. Maybe the shock to my system'll help me forget about yesterday...*

She had woken at first out of a sense of responsibility to the old mare, who would be hungry for her hot morning bran mash. It was Zoey's turn to do chores this morning. She alternated days with her two older sisters. Her little brother Zack was still exempt from the work because he was too young to do it by himself. *Funny how that works,* Zoey thought, *he's too small for barn chores, but not too little to be a pain in my butt...*

She tilted her head up and blew hot air rings into the cold, hungry air. *I love this time of morning,* she sighed, *before anyone else in my family wakes up.* Only the pine trees moved, the backyard stilled by a thin blanket of snow.

Everyone else always seemed afraid of being alone, but for Zoey, time by herself was a rare treat. She could hear herself think without anyone else's voice getting in the way and she didn't have to make polite (or impolite) conversation with her sisters and brother. Alone, she was free to be herself, without worrying about stepping on anyone else's feelings.

"Brrrrr," she shivered, goosebumps having spread over both arms and up her neck. She wrapped her wool jacket tightly around herself now. *Enough of the chill,* she thought, *I hope it warms up soon... winter's been goin' on way too long this year.*

Suddenly something warm dropped onto her shoulder. "Eww...gross!" she cried. "Just my luck." She heard the fluttering of a crow's wings and looked up, covering her face with her hands. *Wouldn't want any of that in my mouth,* she winced. The white splotch stood out against her red and black jacket.

Looking at it, something struck her — *I wonder why bird poop is white when every other animal craps brown? Horse poop's brown, cow poop's brown, goat poop, dog poop, cat poop — they're all brown! So what is it that makes bird poop white? Maybe all that time in the air somehow changes the coloring inside them? Or maybe it's coz of what they eat? But dogs and horses eat different things — one's a carnivore, the other a herbivore — and both have brown doodoo. Nawh, that's not it... Oh, I know! Birds have wings and they flap them. That takes energy. Maybe all the dark stuff inside them gets flapped out?*

As she stepped off the grey concrete walkway behind the garage, her boots sunk into the soggy grass. March rains had already washed away the huge mounds of snow in the backyard and now only small clumps remained. They looked like mini icebergs floating in a sea of green grass and brown dirt.

At the edge of the property, she glimpsed a dark creature standing by a pile of snow. For a second her heart stopped. *Is that a bear?* She watched as it loped toward her. Zoey tensed her body, ready to run back to the safety of the house at any moment. Then she suddenly threw her head back and laughed at her mistake — *not a bear, just Bear.*

"Hey Bear," Zoey called out to the german shepherd, "do ya have ta add your mark on every snow pile ya see?"

At the sound of his name, the big black and brown dog came toward Zoey, brushing her with his bushy tail.

"Oh, you silly dog, I'm just joking," she said, rubbing his head. "Don't take offense. I know you gotta do whatchu gotta do. You're a dog after all."

Bear looked up at her with kind brown eyes, brushed against the side of her leg once more, then led the way across the desolate, pee-stained landscape toward the barn.

The red and white-trimmed, two-story barn looked inviting against the drizzling, grey sky. *A refuge from the rest of the world and most definitely a refuge from my overbearing family,* Zoey thought.

Slosh-thuuuup... slosh-thuuuup... her boots stuck in the mud as she trudged across the yard.

Cruunch... cruunch... their sound changed when she reached the gravel base of the barn.

The barn was a simple structure, built under the supervision of Zoey's dad, with plenty of elbow grease from every member of the family. Zoey remembered how many nails she had pounded that summer. Four hundred seventy-nine in all — she'd counted. A wide gravel path separated two rows of stalls — three on left and one large one on the right, plus the grain room. Each stall had a door at the back that led out to a paddock so the horses could come and go as they chose. A ring of wooden fencing surrounded the barn.

The distinct smell of sweet hay and horse hair mixed with manure greeted Zoey as she slid open the heavy barn door. *Ahhh, home sweet home...* the last bits of her grumpiness evaporated into the musty barn air.

A couple of long flourescent lamps slathered in bird poop hung from the ceiling above the center aisle. Inside the grain room, rows of metal garbage cans sat along one wall, with a plastic, stand-alone sink along the other. A block of wood served as a step stool to wash hands. A bunch of lead ropes and halters hung on hooks against the back wall. A rickety wooden ladder led up to the hayloft, where hundreds of bales lay stacked up to the rafters, which were covered in cobwebs and dust.

"Neighhhhh... neighhhhh..." the horses called out as soon as they heard the door open. Hairy heads poked out curiously above wooden stall doors.

"Okay, okay, I'm comin'... I know you guys are hungry..." Zoey walked down the hallway of the barn patting each horse in turn. Majestic impatiently knocked his front hoof against the stall door. He was a young, bay gelding belonging to her eldest sister. His name suited him — he thought he was royalty and that humans worked for him, not the other way around. *I guess that's kinda true... I mean, who's cleanin' who's poop, after all?*

"Whoa there, take it easy. Gimme a second will ya?"

Quickly entering the grain room, she poured one can each of sweet feed, rolled oats and horse pellets into three well-worn black rubber buckets. As tin lids clanked against their bins and grain spilled into containers, the horses erupted into a chorus of low, muffled whinnies.

"One bucket for you..." Zoey opened Hurricane's stall door and dropped the bucket on the rubber stall mat. The young chestnut mare immediately stuck her head in the bucket and greedily started munching. She belonged to Zoey's second sister.

"And one for you...," she moved to the next stall and gave Majestic a shove as he tried to muscle through her arms for a mouthful of grain before the bucket hit the ground. "Hey, back off, dude. A little patience wouldn't hurt, yunno." Patting him on the shoulder, she laughed... "you're just like me, aren't ya. When you want something, you want it, like — NOW!" Majestic whinnied once, then got down to the business of gobbling up his treat.

"And the last bucket for you, Gypsy," she said to the old bay mare in the largest stall. "How ya doin' this morning ol' girl? Did ya have a good night?"

Gypsy nosed her grain uninterestedly.

"What's the matter? You not hungry this morning?" Zoey was a little surprised by her unusual behavior. "Or do you want your hay first? Savory before sweet?"

Zoey climbed up the ladder from the grain room to the hay loft and threw down a couple bales of hay. At fifty pounds a pop, they weren't easy for a twelve year old girl to handle. But they posed no problem for Zoey with her lean, yet sturdy frame.

Suddenly a white and black creature jumped down from the dusty, cobweb filled rafters and rubbed herself on Zoey's leg.

"Good morning Boots," Zoey smiled, "catchin' some mice are ya?" Zoey stroked her back until Boots purred like a Harley Davidson. "D'ya have a present for me this morning?"

The feline looked at her with silvery green eyes and simply arched her back to draw out Zoey's handstroke. "Hmm, maybe later then? No luck hunting this morning?"
Boots liked to drag her fresh kill into the barn as a gift for whoever did the morning feed.

Zoey dusted bits of hay off her jeans and headed down the ladder back to the grain room. She opened a bale of hay with one expert slice of a utility knife across two orange strings of baling twine and threw three flakes of hay into each of the horses stalls. "Well, that's it guys... enjoy your breakfast. See ya after school..."

As she turned to leave, she heard heavy breathing and snorting coming from Gypsy's stall. She didn't want to disturb the big mare, so she peered quietly over the dirt-encrusted top of the door. Gypsy was standing in the middle of the enclosure, feet splayed wide apart, head down, her muzzle touching the ground. All of a sudden the mare gave a deep grunt, buckled her front knees and collapsed onto her side. Zoey moved stealthily inside the stall and gently patted her on the neck.

"Hey there girl, it's okay, everything will be okay". The mare looked up at her with big brown eyes, at first startled to find her there, then she quietly placed her muzzle in Zoey's hand. "I know you're not feelin' well girl, but I'm here now.... I'll stay with you."   Zoey wasn't wearing a watch, but she knew she'd still have enough time before school because it was one of those rare days she'd woken up her alarm clock.

Gypsy was Zoey's mom's horse from when her mom was a kid. Her mom used to gallop the big mare bareback along the beach, hair and mane streaming in the wind, hoofprints tracking across the sand. Then her mom grew up and didn't ride as much anymore. Gypsy was put out to pasture until her mom decided it was time for Zoey and her siblings to get acquainted with the equine species. They brought the old mare up north. Gypsy survived the two day, eighteen hour drive in the back of a friend's pickup truck. Ropes stabilized her to wooden sides of the rickety vehicle. Since they didn't have a horse trailer, it was the best they could do.

She's a tough old mare, that Gypsy. An unusual mix too — kinda like me. Half draft horse and half Arabian. She has the massive hooves and strong legs of the Clydesdale and the fine facial features of the more delicate Arabian breed. Just like me — a sturdy Scottish lass blended with more delicate Asian features... that's how I like to think of myself... the best of both worlds...

More than anything, Gypsy had a outsized heart. She was a gentle giant. As a baby, Zoey had crawled under the mare's belly while she was eating grass one day. When her mom realized Zoey was missing, she raced madly out of the house only to find her baby perched happily under this two tonne mammoth. One misstep and Zoey would've been toast. Her mom was all freaked out, until Gypsy just turned her head slowly and looked her in the eye as if to say "just chill out... there's nothing to worry about".

Zoey stroked Gypsy's neck and reassured the old mare. Gypsy lay her head down on the sawdust as the barrel of her chest heaved back and forth in large swells, tightening like a drum every few minutes.

Wow, are those what I think they are? Zoey thought excitedly, *I've been waiting for this day for months — eleven months to be exact. I can't believe it's actually here! This musta been goin' on all night, until Gypsy couldn't take it standing up anymore... This is gonna be so cool...*

Just then Gypsy groaned loudly, straining her neck to look

behind her. "Not yet 'ol girl. Keep pushin'... keep pushin'..," Zoey encouraged her as she rubbed the white star on her forehead. Several more minutes went by as Gypsy grunted and snorted, exerting herself forcefully.

Then Zoey spotted it.

Tiny hooves poked out from behind the mare... another push and another... she could see spindly legs now... a few more heaves... now the the tip of a muzzle. Each minute seemed like an hour as Gypsy breathed, dragon-like — nostrils flaring, the whites of her eyes glaring out with the strain of each contraction. With each gigantic heave Gypsy made, a little more of the creature showed.... now the eyes, ears, neck and chest. Not sure whether to run and call someone or stay with the mare, Zoey sat frozen in awe of the spectacle of life unfolding before her eyes. A shiver of excitement tingled down her spine and goosebumps rose all over her arms. What an incredible moment!

Another enormous groan and toughest part was over — the foal's shoulders had passed through the gauntlet. A beautiful baby horse appeared, struggling to breath through the wet amniotic sac still wrapped around it's body. Snapping out of her wonder-filled trance, Zoey sprung into action and stuck her fingers through the plasticky cover near the foal's nostrils.

"There ya go, baby, there ya go... you can breathe easy now," she purred softly to the newborn creature.

Wow...this is a miracle... where did this foal come from? Just grew from a seed in her mama's belly? Grew on what?! Food, water...

Zoey watched as Gypsy licked her foal with long loving strokes... washing off the sticky mucous covering, blood and whatever other bits of goop were stuck on her matted fur.

Wow... that's pure love...

Hey, I know how this baby grew — she fed on love. And now she's here. This little foal's got this feeling about her that's pure innocence, a force field of pure love. Nothing could ever hurt this baby. She's so precious, so beautiful. There must be a power in this universe much greater than our puny little selves, to have produced this amazing creature...

Gypsy whinnied softly at the foal lying next to her, urging her to get up.

"Not a moment to lose, eh Gypsy?" Zoey chuckled. "You're a good mom."

Gypsy continued to lick her newborn baby, washing it with great tongue laps of love. With the sac cleaned off, Zoey could see the foals features — dark brown body, black mane, a white blaze down the face and three white socks on her long, spindly legs. And the most amazing and unusual mark of all... a perfect star right in the middle of her forehead.

Zoey lifted up her hind led — "a girl!"

"Wow, you're a beauty" Zoey gasped in wonder. "You look like a chocolate and vanilla marble cake..."

"Marble... hey, that could work... d'ya like that name?"

Marble stared at Zoey with innocent eyes, gazing right through her. "Oh, you like that name, don't you!?" Zoey said softly, her heart melting. "You're pretty special... Yup, you... slimy wet foal, covered in blood and goop... are the most beautiful creature I've ever seen."

Not wanting to leave, Zoey blew Marble a kiss as she got up out of the stall and made her way back to the house to get ready for school. Little did she know what lay in store for her and this precious newborn foal marked with a perfect star.

4

Crazy Rampage!

RINGGGGG... RINGGGGG... sounded the last bell of the day. Today, it sounded ominous.

"Uh-oh, you know what that means, don't you, Abby?" Zoey said dejectedly. They sat together in the locker room after P.E. class. Her excitement at beating the rest of the grade seven boys at static arm hang changed abruptly with the sound of the bell.

"Yeah, but you don't have to go through with this, yunno," Abby reassured her. "You could just call the whole thing off."

"And let Kev get away with what he did? No way! I've got more self-respect than that."

Pausing, then raising her head with a deep inhale as if gathering her willpower, Zoey continued, "Nope, I can't back out now. I'd be a chicken if I did that. I gotta go through with what I started."

"Okay, suit yourself". Abby shrugged her shoulders.

"Will you come with me though?" Zoey tried to hide the fear lurking inside her with an upbeat voice. "I'd really like you to be there."

"Sure thing," Abby grinned. "I wouldn't miss you kickin' Kev's butt for the world!"

"Glad you're so confident." Zoey pulled on her hole-y jeans and indigo t-shirt. "I'm kinda regretting what I said back there on the stairs yesterday."

"Don't worry, Zoey. You know karate and Kev doesn't. You can swipe him in a second". Abby tossed her head, sending her tangled strawberry blond locks swishing from side to side, emphasizing how much confidence she had in her friend.

"Hah! I bet you wouldn't be so sure if it was you out there. Remember, you're the one who told me to back off right after it happened!" Zoey laughed and grabbed her rusty-orange backpack. "Come on, let's go."

By the time the two girls reached the school parking lot, a crowd of kids had already gathered. Word had spread through the tiny school like wildfire since yesterday. "Somethin's happenin' after school between Kev and Zoey — somethin', like a fight."

Kev was already standing behind the last line of cars, down the embankment, well hidden from view of any teachers, who wouldn't be out to drive their cars home for at least an hour. On the other side of the parking lot the sports field lay empty, bounded by neat rows of houses in the distance. No adults were in sight.

Zoey scanned the crowd nervously and saw a smattering of skin colors. Mattiki was a multicultural community with people from around the world who came to work at the big smelter decades ago — Portugese, Chinese, Indian, British, Greek, Italian, German, Finnish, Filipino and of course Native Indians from the Haisla reservation just a few miles out of town. Forty-one nationalities in all!

Who's side are they on? she wondered silently. *Mine or Kev's? Or maybe no one's?*

Zoey's mixed blood meant she had multiple identities. She didn't conform to any one group. She identified with both the Scottish side from her mom and the Chinese side from her dad. *Eurasian,* she'd been called before she even knew what it meant. Later she learned — European, Asian mix.

Whatever... I don't care who's side they're on. I gotta do what I gotta do. And I don't need anyone else's help. I got myself into this and only I can get myself out.

"I see you've spread word about this," Zoey said as she faced Kev, who stood tall, his blond hair blowing in the chilly breeze. He was surrounded by his friends — Jake on one side, Ryan on the other. A bunch of other boys who desperately wanted be part of their clique, but weren't, stood behind them.

"Yeah, I want the other kids to see me cream you, karate or not," he replied with a cocky smile. "Besides, it's not like fights happen at school every day, yunno. Especially between a guy and a chic. I'm gonna go down in the record books for being the first one to beat a chic at school. And not just any chic. A karate girl."

"Actions speak louder than words Kev," Zoey said calmly, masking her nervousness.

At the sight of Kev, his friends and the gang of kids watching, Zoey's head swirled with doubt. *Is this a big mistake? Will I be able to stand up to this guy, not just with words, but with my fists? Will he beat me up? Will I go home with a black eye and have to explain to my parents that I got into a fight at school? And even worse... that I lost?! If I lose, will all the other kids in the school think I'm a weakling? I've never fought at school before. Can I really use all those moves I learned in the dojo? This isn't practice — it's real life!*

The one-way conversation rattling inside her head was abruptly cut short as Kev moved toward her. The other kids automatically formed a circle around them, like a pack of hyenas surrounding a carcass.

"You think your hands can be registered as lethal weapons, with all your karate training Zoey? SO WHAT. I've been playing sports and wrestling with my brothers my whole life. And in case you haven't noticed, I'm bigger and stronger than you," he laughed mockingly.

His words stung and Zoey felt the hair on the back of her neck rise. *Nothin' like a good taunt to get me goin'*, she thought. *He doesn't realize he's digging his own grave right now. Good thing he can't tell how nervous I am.*

"You've got no idea what you're gettin' yourself into," she replied, feeling her doubts melt away as she spoke these words: "I may be kinda small, kinda quiet and kinda shy, but I'm also kinda TOUGH."

They gave each other the evil eye for a few seconds, in one last attempt to see if the other would back down. Neither of them budged.

It was too late for words now.

Suddenly Kev swung his arm toward her in a fake punch, trying to scare her off. Zoey didn't flinch, knowing she was out of his reach. She had a well-honed sense of distance and timing from sparring with the other orange belts in the karate club.

Hmmph, I guess all those hours in the dojo haven't been for nothing after all...

She was pleasantly surprised by her instinctive response. Although his punch didn't hit her, it acted as a wake-up call. She could feel adrenaline surge through her body as her 'fight response' triggered.

This time Kev closed the distance, aiming to hit her for real. He swung his right arm toward her. She sensed this and quickly stepped off to the right at the last second.

Cool... taisabaki (escape movement) really works, she smiled to herself.

"Whatchu smilin' at?" Kev scowled, annoyed that he missed her. "You just got lucky,"

Zoey locked her eyes on his. Her karate instructor, known as Sensei, once told her: 'when you look someone in the eye, you can tell what they're going to do before they do it. Don't watch the body. Watch the eyes — they give everything away'.

He lunged forward again, this time determined to hit her from the left side, but Zoey spotted a tiny flicker in his eye just before he moved. She twisted her body out of the way and stepped off to the left with her right arm in front of her, blocking his punch. She grabbed his wrist and pulled his arm down in the same direction he punched, redirecting his force so he stumbled forward over the spot where she *was* standing.

"Arrghhh!!! Now you've made me mad," he glared at her.

She sensed his humiliation and played on it, feeling her confidence rise as his fell.

"Still wanna fight, Kev?" she asked with a smirk.

"Hmmph," was his only reply.

This time Zoey didn't wait. She capitalized on her psychological advantage and moved in with a punch to the chest. But Kev also came in with a stomach punch.

WHACK!!!

Their arms collided.

His long, athletic arm hit hers, making her wince. But she recovered quickly... the sharp pain focused her mind like the point of a knife. She backed away, assuming a fighting pose with both fists up, covering her body, ready to strike.

Zoey just had her first taste of being hit by anyone outside the dojo. *Hmm, not so bad. I think I can handle this...*

Kev just had his first taste of being hit by a girl — EVER. *I don't like it, but at least I got her back,* he thought to himself.

"Enough of this," Kev suddenly announced. The humiliation of the fight going on longer than he expected and, with all his friends watching, was gnawing at him. "I'm gonna put an end to this whole thing once and for all," he muttered under his breath.

Jumping forward with his basketball and volleyball strengthened legs, he struck out with his long reach.

WHAM!!!

His punch nailed Zoey on her right side.

She stumbled backward, reeling from the blow — her confidence just as shaken as her ribs.

What just happened? I thought I was winning, dodging all his moves, but now he's got another level I didn't know about? Maybe he's stronger than I thought...?

Doubt crept back into her mind.

Moving forward, partly to banish her doubt, not really

believing in herself, Zoey threw a front kick followed by a face punch. Kev easily saw the half-hearted attack coming, sidestepped it and nailed her on the other side of her body, just below her ribs, harder than before, since Zoey's own momentum compounded the blow.

"OUCH!" she cried, staggering back, clutching her side in pain. 'Never let your opponent know you're hurt', her Sensei had told her, 'it gives them confidence'. *Oh well, so much for that idea*, she groaned inside. Her confidence badly shaken, Zoey's mind started to spin in a negative spiral. *Maybe I should just get out now before I get really hurt? I guess I'm not so good at karate after all...*

Looking around for support, she spotted Abby. Expecting her friend to cheer her on, she noticed Abby looked worried instead. *Oh crap, not a good sign. Come on Abby, gimme some good vibes, will ya?*

Just then, Kev's fist flew into her face, catching her on the left side of her jaw. Clutching her chin and pushing her glasses back onto her nose, Zoey stumbled backward in pain, in complete disbelief that he actually hit her in the face! But even more shocked that he got through her defenses, or lack of them.

With the strike to her jaw, Zoey's fears and doubts instantly morphed into anger. The speed of the transformation shocked even her. She could take blows to the body, but not to the face.

"Don't put your grubby hands on my face! You almost busted my glasses! Now you're gonna get it..."

Instead of caving in, she clenched her teeth and charged forward as if everything depended on it. It was a turning point — she decided this fight would end differently and an unmistakable look of fierce determination came over her. She was so angry, she could feel little beads of sweat pop up all over her skin, even on the backs of her hands.

With ferocious speed, she dealt Kev a front kick to the gut. It caught him off-guard. He had relaxed, thinking the fight was over after the three blows Zoey didn't, or couldn't return.

"Whoa..." he said, shocked by her fury, quickly realizing this was not the same girl he had faced a few seconds earlier.

The house cat had just turned into a TIGER.

With the intense focus of a hunter about to pounce on its prey, she watched him, waiting for the right moment to strike. Thinking he'd better head her off before she gained any more momentum, he attacked. But she beat him to it. With her heightened senses, she sprung forward with a stomach punch and met him in the middle. *The best defense is offense,* she thought, as her punch hit him first. Even though Zoey was smaller, her punch was much faster and therefore stronger.

Force = Mass x Acceleration, she remembered... I may not have much mass, but I sure as heck have acceleration. Besides, I know how to punch with my whole body, not just my arm...

Kev stumbled back, clutching his stomach, sucking wind. "Hey, I didn't know you had that in you Zoey," he said, half-mockingly, hiding his own pain.

"Ready for another?" she asked, her own face still stinging from his blow.

Glancing around at the gang of kids watching them and the boys cheering Kev on, she summoned up every ounce of strength she had. With gritted teeth and clenched fists, she sucked in a deep breath, her inner voice propelling her forward with epic intensity. Without a single sound coming out her mouth, Zoey screamed on the inside...

I AM A **GRRL***!!!!* **HEAR ME ROAR***!!!!*

The incredible strength of her own inner voice sent shivers down her spine. Her eyes narrowed as she lunged toward Kev with her favorite technique — *DOUBLE UP*. A fake punch to the face with the left hand, to make him block and open up, followed by a killer punch to the gut with the right. The full, beautifully synchronized power of her legs, hips, torso, shoulder and arm thrown behind her fist, exploded onto him.

WHAMMMMMMMMM!!!!!!!!!!!!!!!!!!

The force of her punch sent a gasp through the crowd as Kev flew backward, landing on his butt. His eyes popped

out, hands clutching his stomach, mouth open wide, struggling for breath that didn't enter. She had nailed him in the solar plexus, that tender spot just beneath the chest bone where the stomach muscles met, forming a small, unprotected hole.

After what seemed like an eternity, Kev sat up, holding his palm out towards Zoey, barely able to speak. Despite feeling completely humiliated with everyone watching him, he had no choice. The wind and confidence was knocked completely out of him.

"I'm done. You win Zoey," he said quietly, his head hanging down.

"Don't *ever* call me names again," Zoey said with a final, piercing gaze.

5

Cinema Disaster

Luckily, no one knew Zoey had just broken one of the cardinal rules in their household — no fighting outside the dojo. Despite the after school fight, she had made the bus home. And to avoid talking to anyone at home, she'd hidden out in her room until now...

Zoey sat down on the steps to pull on her shoes and wait for her mom to get ready to take her to the theatre. "Mom, could you pleeeease hurry up? I'm gonna be late!" Zoey called from the front door of 37 Rainbow Road.

"Just hold your horses. I'm coming, I'm coming..." Her mom sounded exasperated. "Between the different schedules of all you kids, I feel like a chauffeur!"

"Yeah, whatever," Zoey muttered under her breath, careful not to let her mom hear her — "just hurry up, I can't be late. Abby'll be waiting for me."

Zoey had been careful not to tell anyone at home about

the face off between her and Kev. Although she was proud of having won, she knew that fighting at school wasn't exactly at the top of her parents wish list. Besides, she'd been told by Sensei only to use karate in self-defense, under life-threatening situations.

I was using it in self-defense, she thought. *I was defending my pride, my self-respect... and even if it didn't look like a life and death situation from the outside, it sure felt like it to me...*

Zoey zipped up her jacket and threw on her hood to protect herself against the cold.

'Don't break the rules', mom and dad are always saying... but then they go right-ahead and break them. "No treats after dinner because you already had a sprinkle donut this afternoon. Then my little bro whines a bit and presto! Out come the jellies. 'Just one, okay?' mom says with a stern look on her face. But who's she kidding? One is more than zero and that's the point. Adults are always making rules, then breaking them. What's the point of that? Why have rules at all? Just so you can feel bad about breaking them? Or to give kids something to rebel against? Why not just talk about the reason behind the rule in the first place?

"You're really looking forward to this movie tonight, aren't you Zoey?" her mom said, as she revved up the engine of the big blue bus that was their family car.

"Yeah, kinda". Zoey purposely tried to sound like

she didn't care. Somehow she didn't like the idea of appearing overly excited about anything, as if doing so would give people something over her — because then there'd be something they could take away. But the truth was, she was excited — *hugely*. This was a once a year event and ever since she turned 12 on November 11th, Zoey had been looking forward to it. But, for the rest of the drive into town, Zoey was silent, lost in her own thoughts...

I don't really understand why this can't happen more often. Something dad said about self-discipline??? I'm doing this because I love you? That's the worst — like when they take away my video games or cell phone for a week. What's the 'I love you' part of that?! Why can't they just show their love with a hug or something? Then I'd say sorry, if I've really done something wrong (as opposed to just mischievous). Mom says lots of people love each other but don't really know how to express it. Ever heard of hugs, flowers, chocolate, stuff like that? If you ask me, those are much better ways of showing love than restricting me to only one movie a year... why do my parents have to be so strict when everybody else's aren't?!? No one listens to what I think... Her thoughts spiraled on...

As they pulled up in front of the grey stucco building with a yellow neon sign at the top, Zoey's mom looked over at her for the first time since they left the house. "Here you go Zoey, have a good time. I'll pick you up at 9 pm".

"Thanks mom, see ya later!" Zoey shouted over

her shoulder, as she bounded out the car and up the concrete ramp to the main doors, excited to be allowed to go unsupervised for the first time ever.

As soon as she entered the theatre, she was greeted by the delicious smell of buttery popcorn, sweet licorice and soft drinks. *Umm-hmm, I love the movies*, she thought to herself, drinking in the smells. Abby was nowhere to be seen, so Zoey parked herself on a red bench near the entrance, facing the doors and waited. *I'm a little early, so no wonder she's not here yet. I'm sure she'll show up any minute...*

A few minutes later, as she saw more and more people stream into the theatre, she began to feel a little conspicuous sitting there all by herself.

What if she forgot? Nawh... don't be silly. Abby wouldn't do that. She knows how much I've been looking forward to our only movie night together. She wanted to see this flick too. She'll be here any minute...

More kids walked in, laughing and chatting, including some from her school. When they saw Zoey sitting there, they stared and whispered to each other. She knew they were talking about her and could imagine what they were saying... *hey, isn't she the one who beat Kev in a fight earlier today? Wow, that's pretty cool, especially for a girl. She must be strong...*

Imagining them talking about her like that in her mind made Zoey feel bigger, more powerful. She raised her chin slightly and sat up a bit straighter. But a few minutes later she began to fidget in her seat, looking at her watch. Ten past seven. *Abby's late. I hope she gets here soon, the show's gonna start in ten minutes.*

Zoning out, trying to distract herself from the ticking clock, she daydreamed about how she and Abby had first met:

* * *

Standing in front of her new grade three class, Zoey felt her knees wobble. She scanned the room, looking for friendly or familiar faces and saw none.

Why is everyone staring at me like I'm from another planet? I just came from across town! Hey, wait a minute, there's a friendly face. Yeah, that strawberry blonde girl near the back row, smiling at me. Whew! And there's an empty desk next to her — great! I'll sit there...

"Hi, I'm Zoey". She plunked herself down, dropping her backpack to the floor, glad to be out of the uncomfortable spotlight as newbie in the class.

"Howdy, welcome to Eagle. I'm Abigail, but you can call me Abby for short."

They clicked from the start. They just seemed to *get* each other. Zoey had her sisters and brother of course, but that was different — they were family. She and Abby *chose* to be friends.

"Abby, I love your life," Zoey told her as they got to know each other.

"Why?"

"Coz you live in town. I envy your city life — well, small town life."

"What're you talking about?" Abby lifted one side of her mouth in disbelief that anyone could envy a life she thought was pretty average. Maybe even less than average.

"You live two blocks from school, one block from the corner-store and three blocks from the ice cream shop. I mean, what could be better than that?!"

"You dunno what 'ur talkin' about," Abby shook her head.

Zoey waved her off and continued, "you don't have to rush out of the house every morning to catch the bus, or wait for it after school. You can even go home for lunch instead of eating cold sandwiches out of a paper bag like me."

"Are you kidding?" Abby looked shocked. "I'd looooove to eat lunch at school, but my mom *makes* me come home for lunch. She says she misses me by lunch time and wants to eat with me. I'd much rather eat with my friends, cold food or not."

"Oh well, at least you get to pop by the corner-store for an ice cream anytime you want, rather than waiting for your mom to go to the grocery store." Zoey raised her eyebrows for confirmation.

"You're dreamin'! I'm not allowed to have ice cream whenever I want. I still have to ask and mom rarely says 'yes'!" Abby threw up her arms in frustration. "You have no idea girl!"

"You're the one with an awesome life, Zoey. Living on a farm with horses, tons of space and all those animals — even a gym in your basement for heaven's sake! Life's so unfair," she pouted.

"You think it's fun to shovel manure before coming to school?" Zoey snorted. "I gotta make sure I haven't got any on my clothes before I board the bus, otherwise I'll stink up the class! Then no one'll want to be my science partner — not even you!" They both burst out laughing...

* * *

Snapping back to reality, Zoey looked at her watch again. 7:15 pm.

Where is she? This is really strange. I wonder if she's okay? Should I call her house? Nawh... I don't want to bother her folks. She'll be here soon. Be patient, just be patient, Zoey.

Five minutes later, Zoey started to feel embarrassed sitting by herself for so long when everyone else was with friends. To top it off, just at that moment, a few more kids from her school showed up, looked at her, then walked off talking in hushed tones. Her mind started spiraling down like a rapidly draining bathtub as she imagined them saying nasty things about her now:

She thinks she's so tough, picking a fight with someone at school just to show off her karate skills. She really went out of

~ 56 ~

her way to humiliate that guy when all he did was call her a name. I mean, he used words and she just lost it on him. Way out of proportion. Kinda mean, actually. I'd stay away from her if I were you...

To escape her negative thoughts, Zoey stood up, pacing back and forth in front of the doors, scanning for Abby's face. She didn't see her, so her mind continued to swirl downwards. The bathtub was almost completely drained now... then she stopped in her tracks.

Abby's not late or hurt, she suddenly realized! She forgot about me! Darn it! Doesn't she care? Doesn't she take our friendship seriously? She knew how much I was looking forward to this. One movie a year?!? I mean, how can you not show up for that! How thoughtless of her. This is just like that worried look she gave me yesterday during the fight — totally unsupportive. True friends don't do that to each other. Oh boy, am I gonna give her a piece of my mind when I see her!

Disappointed, hurt and tired of the depressing images flashing on the screen of her own mind, Zoey entered the theatre by herself to watch the film playing on the other screen, the big screen that everyone had paid to come and see.

That night, Zoey went to bed with an awful feeling in the pit of her stomach. The imaginary movie about how little Abby cared about her still played in her mind, leaking into her dreams.

At school the next day, she spotted Abby in the hallway.

"Hey, how come you weren't there last night? I waited for you and you didn't show up. You stood me up!" Zoey wailed. Her voice was sharp with hurt and anger. A dangerous combo — sad and mad at the same time.

"Whoa... Chill out girl. Why're you so angry? You have no idea what happened with me."

Just say sorry Abby, Zoey's mind raced. Just say sorry and say that you'll make it better. Then everything'll be alright. I don't wanna get into another fight, I just wanna know that you care about me!

Instead of saying her thoughts out loud, Zoey said something else. Angry words poured out of her mouth.

"You weren't there! You knew how much I was looking forward to it and you just didn't show. How could you do that to me?!" she shouted.

"Wait a sec. Yes, I did know how desperate you were to see this movie," Abby said defensively.

"I wasn't desperate. I just needed to do something to get my mind off the fight with Kev."

"Whatever," ," Abby rolled her eyes, angry herself now. "Will you let go of that already?"

"You said you wanted to see this film too, Abby. Did you change your mind or something?" Zoey asked sarcastically.

"No. I got my period again and had really bad cramps

this time! But I guess you wouldn't know about that, would you?! I tried ringing you but my phone was out of juice."

"Well... that's not good enough. Good friends are there for each other. They don't just NOT show up!" Zoey smoldered.

"You don't have to be so upset Zoey," Abby grumbled.

"WELL I AM! GO FIND ANOTHER FRIEND TO GO TO THE MOVIES WITH NEXT TIME IF YOU CAN'T EVEN SHOW UP!"

"OK, FINE! I WILL!" Abby shouted defiantly. "You're not my friend either, SEE YA!" Surprised by her ultimatum and fed up with the torrent of angry words Zoey had been spewing at her, Abby stormed off.

Zoey watched her best friend walk away, staring after her with daggers in her eyes and a hole in her heart.

6

Anger Issues

Running home from the bus-stop after school, Zoey slammed the front door and kicked off her shoes as she entered the house.

"Wassup, Zoey," called her little brother Zack, who was sitting at the kitchen table eating chocolate chip cookies.

"Never mind. Just leave me alone," she replied in a surly voice, dropping her backpack by the door and opening the fridge.

"Whoa. Somethin's eatin' you up." He stared at her with his eyebrows raised in alarm. "Had a bad hair day?"

"I said LEAVE-ME-A-LONE. What part of that don't you understand?" Zoey turned to look at her brother who was 10, only two years younger than her. They were about the same size, but she still carried an authority over him that he didn't challenge — at least, not yet.

"I'm outta here. Don't wanna be around miss

grumperstiltskin." He grabbed his plate of cookies and left the kitchen.

Hmm, I need something sweet to make me feel better... Nothing in the fridge. Let me try the freezer. Bingo! Apple turnovers from Jill's bake shop. Deee-lishhh!

Feeling better after her snack, Zoey headed upstairs to her room — the first one on the left, across from the bathroom. She closed her door and pulled her favorite book out of her backpack thinking she'd curl up on her carpet and read. But a few minutes later she fidgeted uncomfortably, got up and started rummaging through her messy closet. She soon dropped that and started shuffling papers around on her desk.

Nothing works. Nothing's making me feel better, she thought to herself.

Zoey looked around her room. A pile of dirty clothes lay behind the door, with others strewn around the room. Books and papers were scattered across her desk and shelf, spilling onto the floor next to the waste basket. A harmonica and small, cheap guitar sat at the foot of her bed, underneath a large window. Her walls were bare except for a poster of a girl galloping bareback on a horse that said "RIDE like a girl" and another poster of a duckling who'd fallen into a bucket. It said: "some things are easier to get into than to get out of".

She scanned the mess, thinking... *maybe I'll clean my*

room. Mom's always asking me to do that. But wait... what's the big deal about keeping all your stuff tidy anyhow? Seriously, it's just gonna get messed up again! All that time I spend cleaning up markers and papers, putting clothes back on hangers, books on shelves, I could've been doing something fun! I tried that argument on mom, except I changed 'fun' to 'doing homework or practicing piano'. Hmmph, she didn't buy that one. She just raised an eyebrow at me. Yunno, that one raised eyebrow look of 'yeah, right...', with the corner of her mouth turned up too, as if she's saying 'you really think I'm gonna believe that'?

Well, mom's not home to make me tidy up — she's still at work. And Dad's holed up in the office downstairs with the door shut. That means DO NOT DISTURB. Maybe I'll go outside. I know — I'll go see Marble. She'll cheer me up. Zoey headed downstairs, put on her gum-boots, worn wool jacket and sloshed out to the barn.

She could feel the fresh air clear her head as soon as she stepped outside.

Peering over the edge of Gypsy and Marble's stall, she saw Marble nursing from her mother. Zoey slid the black cast iron latch open and entered the stall.

"Hey ol' girl, how you doin' today?" Zoey asked the mare, as the big horse walked over and nuzzled her. Zoey rubbed her forehead, twisting Gypsy's black forelock around her fingers.

"I'm not doing too well," Zoey said, sad and confused. "Everything's been going all wrong the last few days. And now Abby and I aren't friends anymore." Zoey hugged Gypsy around her thick hairy neck, soaking in her warmth and unconditional love. "Can you help me make things right?"

The big mare blew her nose, sending greeny-brown, wet, sticky horse mucous flying everywhere.

"Hey, is that how you show your love? Spraying snot on me?" Zoey laughed. "You're a funny one, Gypsy — and I love you for it." *I'm so glad Mom introduced me to you.*

Marble peeked out cautiously from behind her mother's rear-end.

"Hey cutie. Wow, you are just adorable, with your white star, blaze and three white stockings on your spindly little legs."

Marble stomped her feet, as if she knew what Zoey was talking about.

"Don't worry, you'll grow into those legs. Baby horses always do, just like baby dogs grow into their paws and baby humans grow into their heads. I had a pretty big, ugly head when I was born. Not that your legs are ugly. That's not what I meant."

Marble flared her nostrils at Zoey, still wary of humans at just a couple days old.

"Well, you're a beauty, that's for sure."

As if agreeing with Zoey, Marble raised her head.

"Come here gal, I just wanna pet you," Zoey cooed, stretching her hand out towards the foal.

When Marble didn't budge, Zoey started to move closer, but the little foal backed away.

"Still shy are ya?" Zoey smiled, "even after I saw you come outta your mama the other day? That was pretty cool... for you too, eh?"

"Oh, I know what you'll like," Zoey said as she disappeared from the stall. She returned with a handful of grain.

"This is like a chocolate bar to you guys, isn't it?!" She held her open palm toward Marble but Gypsy was faster. The big mare licked the treat out of Zoey's hand with her wet, course tongue, slurping up every bit of grain and even catching pieces that were stuck between Zoey's fingers.

"Hey, you weren't supposed to do that! That was for your baby, you big pig!" Zoey swatted at the old mare playfully. Gypsy just nodded her head excitedly and whinnied for more.

"All right, all right, I'll get you some." Zoey grabbed a bucket from the grain room and dumped a scoop of horse pellets in it, returning to the stall with the prize.

As she opened the door, Gypsy planted her muzzle in the bucket greedily, using her strong head to push through Zoey's arms. Zoey had just enough time to grab a fistful of grain before it all disappeared.

Marble followed her mom closer to the door, still a healthy distance from Zoey, watching her curiously.

"Clk, Clk, here girl, I've got a treat for ya," Zoey called gently, clucking her tongue off the roof of her mouth the way she'd seen her mom do.

Marble stayed put.

Zoey called her again, this time a little more forcefully. "Come on girl, cut me some slack, will ya." She waited a moment, then realized the grain trick wasn't working.

Suddenly, she had a bright idea...

Zoey grabbed a brown leather halter and blue lead rope from the tack room and returned, hiding both behind her back so Marble couldn't see them.

"Hey Marble, it's me again, I've still got something for ya," Zoey beckoned, stretching out her other hand, filled with grain.

A little more confident now that some time had passed, Marble reached out her neck to sniff Zoey's hand. *Oh, she's so velvety soft... if I could only pet the rest of her, but I still can't reach...*

Just then, Zoey made her move.

She threw the rope over Marble's neck and held it tight. Startled by the unknown thing around her neck, Marble lunged back and felt the rope pull down on her. The pressure scared her even more and she lurched back again, hitting the stall wall with her hocks.

BOOM!

The loud sound triggered the filly's *fight* or *flight* instinct, a protective mechanism all horses are born with — either flee or fight in the face of something dangerous. But with nowhere to escape, she raised her front legs to strike out in protection. Zoey was startled by Marble's unexpected response and jumped back to avoid flying hooves, dropping the lead rope.

"Whoa girl, whoa… it's okay. I'm not gonna hurt ya — I just wanted to get close to you."

Wide-eyed and terrified, Marble stood shaking in the corner of the stall. The halter and lead rope lay uselessly on the sawdust.

"Oh, I'm sorry girl… I'm so sorry. I didn't mean to scare you. I just wanted to hold you."

As Zoey stepped forward to collect the rope from the ground, Marble bolted to the other corner of the stall.

"Oh great. Now I've scared you off too!" Zoey cried. "I can't take this anymore. Everything's just going horribly wrong!"

Running back to the house, feeling even more upset than when she first came out, Zoey was an emotional wreck. Rage, frustration and sadness all mixed inside her, forming a soup of bad feeling.

What should I do? I feel awful. I just wanna get this terrible feeling outta me. But how? No one else seems to be able to help me — not even the horses. Maybe I'll just go downstairs and be alone..."

She trudged down to the dark, cool basement and parked her butt along the far wall, sitting on a light green tatami mat that formed part of their home karate gym. A wide, full-length mirror was attached to the wall at one end of the room, a large punching bag at the other end. Her head cupped in her hands, she started sobbing. Her whole body shook with the pain of the past few days. Everything that could possibly go wrong was going down the toilet, fast... spiraling totally out of control.

Suddenly Zoey looked up, her face wet with tears. She stared at the punching bag and jammed her fists on her knees.

That's it. I need to hit something and get this frustration outta me. I need to pound something — hard! As she stood up, her head spun.

What happened the last few days? I'm fighting with everyone. How can everything go sooo bad, sooo fast?!

She stumbled over to the punching bag.

WHAM!

Her right fist dug into the hard brown leather. *First, I fight with my parents, telling them I want to quit karate and piano lessons...*

BAM!!

Her left fist made another indent. *Then the fight with Kev after school yesterday...*

SMACK!!

Two hands hit simultaneously and sent the bag swinging in the opposite direction. *Then the argument with Abby at school today...*

WHAM!!!

She threw her whole torso onto the bag, sending it spinning in a circle. *And now Marble. I shouldn't have tried to force her to let me pat her. What was I thinking?!?!*

Is it me or everyone else? What's wrong with me? Can't I get along with anyone? Everything's going wrong! I am soooo miserable right now. Why does my life suck so much!!!

SLAMMM!
SLAMMM!!
SLAMMM!!!

She hit the bag with her fists and arms, releasing the rage that boiled inside her, burning up her insides. Her body was moving erratically and out of control. Sparks flew off the hard brown leather worn from years of blows.

Something's gotta change. I can't keep going like this. I don't care about anyone or anything. I just want to feel better. I just want to get rid of this anger and replace it with something else, anything else... anything's gotta be better than this!

Heaving sobs, alternating with enraged screams, erupted

from her as she continued to flail against the heavy bag. It swung violently from side to side, almost unhinging the silver chain attaching it to the ceiling beam overhead.

As she thrust her limbs onto the bag again and again, the POWW! POWW! POWW! sound of her fists started to form a rhythm... An erratic beat at first, slowly evening out as Zoey started to tire, as if the steady hand of fatigue were forcing her to find her natural rhythm. The anger inside her eased and her body started flowing with the punches. She took one step away from the bag and used her reach and technique, as well as pure force, allowing years of martial arts training to kick in. As she stepped back from the tight grip of her anger, a lightbulb went off in her head.

AHA! I know what I want — RELIEF! That's it! Relief from my feelings. Relief from my negative thoughts. Relief from my rage! I've got to find a better way...

One, two, three punches...

Instead of wild slams, her punches became focused laser beams. Her fingers clenched tight, fists sliding against her side, wrists turning to align with fully-extended arms just at the point of contact.

Eleven, twelve, thirteen...

She was building speed and power with every punch now, getting into the flow...

Thirty-four, thirty-five, thirty-six...

She was really getting letting loose now, slowly easing into the zone...

sixty-seven, sixty-eight, sixty-nine...

Suddenly, it happened. Something changed.

Imperceptible at first, Zoey realized something felt different. She was actually *enjoying* hitting the bag now. She liked the feeling of strength generated from the tork of her hips, shoulders and arm releasing pent-up energy in one smooth, synchronized motion, each time her clenched fists flew out.

Hey, this feels good. I'm strong. I'm really good at this.

Each time her fist connected with the bag, swinging it far in the opposite direction, the feeling of power grew inside her.

I can really hit hard — I love this!

She stopped for a moment, felt her heart pounding in her chest and realized her anger had settled. With each punch, a little anger had dissolved away, a little more power seeped in.

She actually felt *good... powerful... strong.*

A few more punches later, she didn't even feel angry anymore.

Hey, I like this feeling. I like feeling that I'm in charge of my world, not trapped by what's happening to me.

I like it, I love it, I want some more of it...
I like it, I love it, I want some more of it...
I like it, I love it, I want some more of it...

she chanted to herself...

Her arms hanging down, she stepped away from the bag and sat down in the corner of the dojo, drained and elated at the same time. The ferocity of her rage had taken everything out of her, like sucking the last bit of juice out of a juice box, the plastic sides caving into nothingness. Physically exhausted from the more than two hundred and sixty times she had pounded on the bag, her body went limp as she slumped against the wall. The leather punching bag swung slower and slower until the only thing moving in the room was her chest, heaving up and down, sucking in the basement's stale air.

Somewhere deep inside her, something had clicked. A little light had switched on — at first a flicker, then with each punch a stronger glow.

Something had shifted inside her when she broke past the mental barrier of actually hitting a target as hard as she possibly could. When she fully unleashed herself on the punching bag and felt her own powerful force against the hard leather surface.

Something shifted as she channelled ANGER to POWER. It was like a lid had been removed.

The anger in Zoey had lifted and created and new, open space within her.

She took a few deep breaths, stood up and went to check out the smell of curried chicken that wafted under her nose - her Dad's yummy cooking - mixing with the smell of sweat and elation. Climbing the stairs, she felt a strange yet satisfying sense of accomplishment, power... and relief.

Zoey had just turned her *PAIN* into *PROMISE*.

Without realizing it, she'd done something that would change her life forever. She had stumbled on a way of transforming *FEAR* into *LOVE*.

7

Keep your head on... what the #*@!?

Zoey walked up the steps from the basement. In a daze from her newfound discovery that she could turn her anger into a good feeling, she nearly bumped into her short, Chinese grandma, (they called her "Ama"), who was coming the other way, descending from upstairs, slowly and carefully placing two feet on each step. As they both reached the ground floor, they spotted each other and entered the kitchen together.

Ama had lived most of her life in China and now that she was old and didn't want to live alone, she'd be staying with Zoey's family for awhile. Since Ama had been living with them the last three months, they'd been eating a lot better — freshly cooked food most nights, unlike the frozen TV dinners or mass produced weekend chili's they had received before.

Ama would be staying indefinitely and as far as Zoey was concerned, that was just fine. After all, she slept with Zoey's eldest sister in her room and didn't bother anyone much. Although she was quiet, Ama was unusually spry and quick-witted for a short, wrinkled, old woman.

"Hi Ama," Zoey chirped.

Although six times her age, Ama was still the same height as Zoey.

Funny how people shrink as they get older, Zoey chuckled. *Ama never was tall, but at least she used to be taller than me. I'm not growing that fast. Gravity must be doing a number on her.*

"Hi Zoey, good to see you. Where you been hiding since you come home from school? I not seen you yet today," Ama said in broken English, with a toothless grin erupting from below her round owlish glasses.

Another weird thing about old people — they lose their teeth, just like six year olds... and how come they always have the most nerdy specs?

Zoey tried to ignore the useless chatter in her head.

"Oh, yunno... just had stuff to do," Zoey said, busily rubbing her nose. She tried to avoid getting drawn into details about her argument with Abby and clash with Marble, not to mention her most recent episode on the punching bag.

The kitchen was filled with the delicious aroma of curried coconut chicken and steaming jasmine rice. A large window overlooking the front yard sat above the sink, surrounded by a wrap around counter broken up only by a white fridge on one side and a stove on the other. A silver dishwasher with a wooden top served as island and chopping block. The counter was littered with various utensils, pasta jars, papers, junk and a rice cooker boiling away in one corner beside a steaming wok. An old wooden table with six spindled chairs sat at the other end of the kitchen. That's where they ate most of the time, except for special occasions like birthdays, or when guests came over. A large, carved, antique wooden table with eight high-backed Scottish chairs sat elegantly in the dining room, just beyond the more simple, practical furniture of the kitchen.

Yumm...my favorite dinner, thought Zoey. *I love having Ama here coz we don't have to eat noodle soup made with whatever leftovers are in the fridge, cooked in five minutes flat...*

"You help set table, okay Zoey?" Ama said, peering at her.

"Yeah, sure."

As Zoey reached up to grab some cups from the cupboard, Ama spotted a dark purply-brown bruise on her face.

"What that?" Ama pointed to Zoey's jaw. "You fall down or something?"

"Uh... uh...," *should I just make something up?* Zoey's mind raced. But looking at her grandma's gentle face yet piercing eyes, she decided against it. *Just tell the truth. Ama's too smart - she'll see right through it, like she did the last time I tried to cover something up... and then I got in even worse trouble...*

Zoey looked down, pausing for a moment. "No, I didn't fall down Ama. I got into a fight," she confessed.

"Fight?! You sparring in dojo?"

"No. At school."

"Aieyaahhh! Not supposed to fight at school." Ama wagged her finger at Zoey.

Great. I knew this would happen. I shoulda kept my mouth shut. Now I'm gonna get an earful...

"What happen?" Ama asked sternly.

"Uh... uh... nothing, really. It was nothing."

"What HAPPEN?" Ama asked again, raising her voice slightly.

Realizing her grandma was not prepared to let this subject go until she got a full account, Zoey reluctantly uncorked the bottle inside where she suppressed and stored all emotionally charged experiences.

With a sigh, she explained as briefly as possible. "This boy at school called me a name, so I punched him. He said he wouldn't ever call me names again."

Hey maybe this isn't so bad — telling Ama. Explaining it like that makes me feel kinda proud of how I did out there. Kev deserved it, after all. Not just because of what he said to me, but for all those other kids who didn't fight back. I was right to fight.

"What he call you?" Ama was obviously not going to settle for a one line answer.

"IDIOT."

"What that mean?" She was genuinely puzzled.

"Yunno... like... dumb, but a really not nice way to say it. Not that there is a nice way..." Zoey's voice trailed off...

"So that's it? You punch him one time and he go down?" Ama's eyes opened wide in amazement.

"Well, not exactly," Zoey explained, amused that her grandma was interested in the details of the fight.

"We started by staring each other down with lots of other kids standing around in a circle. When neither of us would back down, he threw out a couple punches, but I just moved out of the way. I used the escape techniques we learned in karate class. He didn't like that, so he tried to hit me harder."

"What you do then?"

"We both attacked and hit each other. I hurt my arm, but it only made me more focused," Zoey explained, starting to feel pretty good about herself, carefully setting seven red plastic dragon plates around the table.

"Yes — pain make mind sharp," Ama nodded her head as she wiped down the counter.

"Then he hit me hard, in the ribs. And I got hurt," Zoey remembered, wincing. "I lost my confidence and he hit me again, this time in the face."

"Oooo... not good," Ama pursed her wrinkled lips.

"When he hit me in the face, I lost it. I went crazy, like a tiger you know?! I hit him as hard as I could — twice. He fell on the ground and couldn't breath. That's when he asked me to stop."

"Hmm... you went crazy — like madwoman? Only body? No mind? Not good... not good..." Ama said, shaking her head. "You must always keep your head — always."

Huh?! Whatchu talking about Ama? Keep my head? What's that supposed to mean?

"What do you mean Ama — **keep my head?**" Zoey asked respectfully, notching up the politeness level before the words escaped her mouth.

Mom and dad are always talking about being polite, she remembered. *They say it's a sign of respect. What does that word mean anyway?*

R-E-S-P-E-C-T. They say it means caring for others in your family, but I think it means RESident insPECTion, coz whenever I stop showing respect they grill me about who I've been hanging out with...

Ama lifted the lid of the rice cooker to see if the grains were cooked, thinking about Zoey's question. Then she started talking again. "*Keep your head.* That mean you not use fist if not have to. Words more powerful than fist sometimes. Always use words first. Try not fight."

What?! What am I learning karate for then? Why am I doing hundreds of kicks and punches every week in the dojo? Just for the fun of it? Uh....NOT!

"What do you mean Ama, 'try not fight'? I was mad and he deserved it." Zoey filtered the voice in her head through a more polite tongue, even though she was becoming increasingly impatient.

"Karate for defense, not offense," Ama said calmly. "Violence last resort only. Diplomacy better."

Diplomacy? Huh?!? I've never even heard that word before. I don't even know what it means. Since when am I supposed to use diplomacy instead of karate?!? Besides, I was defending myself. I was defending my honor, my pride, my self-respect.

"Whatever, Ama," Zoey mumbled in frustration. "I'll look up diplomacy in the dictionary..." She pulled out the cutlery drawer and started fumbling through spoons and forks...

"I not say *'not fight'*. I say *'try* not fight'. Ama put her hand on top of Zoey's fistful of forks. "If words not work, then okay use fists. More expected of you since you study karate. You karate girl." Ama's eyes glistened with the wisdom of decades of martial arts study herself. It ran in the family — she'd studied wushu with the monks in the temples near her home village in rural China. Something very unusual for a girl in those days. But Zoey didn't know any

of those stories about Ama... yet.

You don't get it Ama. And Kev certainly wouldn't have gotten it either. I mean, he was the one who started it in the first place. He crashed into me, called me names and I didn't do anything to him except share the same stairway!

Speechless, Zoey just stared at Ama in disbelief, then pulled her hand away.

Sensing her defensiveness, Ama said quietly but firmly— "**Inner strength** Zoey. Karate not about punching and kicking. About building inner strength."

What?!?! Coulda fooled me. I musta done a thousand punches and kicks over the years, since I started karate at age five. But wait a sec... I did have a moment when I wondered whether I shoulda just let his comment go... Was that inner strength?

"Fear and inner strength very different," she continued, as if reading Zoey's mind. "Both make you not fight. But for *very* different reason."

"So am I supposed to just let people push me around? Then what am I learning karate for anyway?" Zoey laid the metal implements around the table, feeling bewildered.

"No, Zoey. Not let people push you around. That's fear," she explained slowly, her eyes narrowing as she looked right through Zoey. "It take strong person to be gentle. **The stronger you are on inside, more gentle you can be on outside.** When someone try to make you angry, don't. Just stay calm. That's strong person."

"I was calm, Ama — " Zoey threw her arms out, exasperated and fed up with this twisted, confusing conversation. "I could've punched him out right there — but I *didn't*. I waited till the next day to do it." A sly smile crept over Zoey's face as she turned away from Ama and reached for the knives.

Ignoring Zoey's cheeky remark, Ama continued, "other people like *mirror* for you Zoey. When you angry at them, you angry at yourself. They only show you what's going on inside you. You always get back same energy you put out. Don't blame others... use as mirror to reflect back on you instead. You think about what inner strength mean to you Zoey. Think about mirror." With that final comment, she picked up a ladle to stir the simmering curry.

"Okay Ama, I'll think about it," Zoey muttered, feeling completely misunderstood. She rolled her eyes at the back of her grandma's head as she lay knives and forks around the kitchen table.

8

I'm Sorry...

"I'm stuffed," Zoey groaned. She looked expectantly across the table at her mom, hoping to get a reprieve from the steadfast rule of the Lee household that you must wait for everyone to finish before leaving the table.

All these silly rules adults make up... like sitting at dinner till everyone's finished... I mean, what's the point of that?! After my tummy's full, I just wanna let the blood rush to my stomach to digest my food, preferably horizontally. But nooo, gotta wait for the slow pokes to eat, especially my little brother, who chews every bite, like, thirty-two times! I swear, even a cow chewing her cud chews less than he does... mom says those are good manners, but dad doesn't really seem to care. He burps after every meal — says it's a Chinese custom. Something about a sign that the meal was delicious?...wow, that really drives mom crazy...

Zoey leaned back in her chair, the worn wooden spindles

wobbly from years of kids rocking them back and forth — tonight was no exception...

Oh yeah and then when I'm done, I have to say 'may I be excused please?' As if patiently waiting for eternity weren't enough, I still have to politely ask permission to leave?! Honestly, what difference does it make if I just eat, get up, park myself on the couch and join the dinner conversation from there? I promise not to play nintendo or text my friends on my cell phone... But mom's adamant about this rule. Funny, coz there aren't many things she's adamant about...except having her coffee in the morning and her car keys being left in the bowl by the door...guess I'd better sit this one out and just wait... not worth testing her patience at the end of the day when she's already tired and worn out.

"May I be excused please?" Zoey asked a few minutes later.

"Sure, we're all done." Her mom nodded at her.

Zoey dropped her plate in the sink, went to her room and closed the door. From the comfort of her floor, she stared out at the starry night sky. Ama's words swirled in her head:

'Other people like mirror for you...'

'Inner strength...'

'Strong on inside, gentle on outside...'

None of that makes any sense to me. I wish I knew what Ama was talking about...

Rolling over, she spotted something shiny on the floor

behind her desk. *Hey, isn't that the thing Ama gave me for my birthday last year? What's it doing there? Must've fallen off my desk...*

She reached over and picked up the emerald green stone, carefully holding it in the palm of her hand, smoothing the finely chiseled edges with her fingers. *I love this rock... it's such a beautiful color and it looks amazing in the light.* As she held it up to the moonlight, she noticed how the brilliant white glow of the full moon reflected off the stone into her room, creating a swarm of dancing silver butterflies on the ceiling. "Cool..." she exclaimed breathlessly, turning the stone like a puppeteer, making the butterfly dance appear even more dazzling.

Then it dawned on her — *moonlight, reflected, becoming butterflies. The stone is like a mirror, just like Ama was saying other people are for me. A mirror reflecting the moonlight, making it look different... Huh? So if someone's a mirror for me, they make me look different?*

She cocked her head sideways to look at her reflection in the floor length mirror against her wall. *But I look the same in the mirror...*

Then she spotted a glow in her eyes she hadn't seen before...

Wait a minute, I get it... maybe mirrors just make me see myself differently, but I'm really the same person? The moonlight is still moonlight, it just looks like butterflies... I'm still me, I just appear angry or calm...

Zoey rolled over onto her stomach, laying her head in her hands.

I'm still so confused. Maybe writing in my journal will help me sort it out.

She reached for a small, yellow, spiral bound notebook on her shelf.

Grabbing a pen, she wrote:

1. Ama said 'other people are like a mirror.' So if you're angry at someone, they're showing you that you're angry at yourself. What the...? Okay, I don't really get this, but let's just go with it for now...

2. Angry at Kev = Angry at Zoey.
   So, when I was mad at Kev, it meant I was really mad at myself?
   But he deserved my anger! He was a jerk! Okay, get over it Zoey. Take another example. What about what happened today in the barn?

3. Angry at Marble = Angry at Zoey.
   When I was mad at Marble, I was mad at myself? This one actually makes sense. Marble didn't do anything to make me mad at her. She was just hanging out in her stall, then I came in and tried to put the lead rope on her. It was all my fault that it went bad.

4. Anger ≠ Love. If I'm angry at myself, I feel bad. And that means I don't have much love in me.

5. ++ **Love**. I want to feel good. I need more love inside me.

How am I supposed to get more love? From others? There's not a whole lot going around in our house. From myself? How do I do that? Wrap my arms around myself and give me bear hugs? Look in the mirror and say 'I love you Zoey, I really, really love you. You're alright girl?' That just seems stupid and corny. And if I do that anyway, will things really get better? How can that possibly affect my relationship with Marble?

Zoey put her pen down and rested her head in her palms, staring out her window.

I dunno if this stuff works. Maybe it'll be clearer in the morning...Yeah, clear as mud, she laughed to herself. *I'll just sleep on it...*

She changed into her baggy cotton PJ's, took off her golden rimmed glasses, laid them carefully on her desk and crawled into bed. She was quite happy to stare at the back of her eyelids after an emotionally exhausting day.

The next morning, Zoey woke up feeling better, as if a weight had lifted. She jumped out of bed full of energy, looking forward to school, thinking about what she'd written in her journal the night before.

As she was brushing her teeth, a thought struck her like a thunderbolt. She stood staring at herself in the mirror, mouth full of foam —

Wait a minute. If Kev is a mirror for me, then Abby is too! I wasn't really mad at Abby for not showing up at the

theatre. I was mad at myself?!
  Nawh... she really stood me up...
  Well, maybe I did overreact a little... she had a reason for not being there. She had bad cramps, remember? Was I a little hyped up after the whole fight with Kev and everything?

  An hour later, heading towards math class, Zoey spotted her friend in the hallway.
  "Hey Abby," she called, picking up her pace.
  "Hey Zoey". Abby's response was cool at best.
  The two friends stood face to face in the middle of the bustling hallway. Finally, Zoey raised her eyebrows, took a deep breath and threw up her arms, sputtering out, "wanna be friends again? I'm sorry about how I treated you the other day."
  "Hmmph. You sure get all hot and bothered sometimes, yunno Zoey. Don't get so worked up next time..."
  "Yeah, I know," Zoey cast her eyes down, a little embarrassed at her passionate outburst. "I over reacted. That's just my style — all hot and bothered. I'm working on it... I'm working on it..."
  Abby gazed down the hall, avoiding Zoey's eyes.
  "Well, I'm really sorry. I shouldn't have shouted at you," Zoey said.
  Abby looked up. "Hmm, let's see, should I be your friend...?" she teased, holding her index finger to her lips for emphasis.

"Yeah, I guess so. I still like ya... you'll do."

"Awesome! You're the best Abby," Zoey said as she wrapped her arms around her friend.

"Does this mean you'll come to my birthday sleep over?"

"Sure thing — wouldn't miss it for the world," Zoey grinned.

9

Patience Zoey, Patience...

Hopping down from the bus, Zoey ran home thinking of what had happened at school.

Ama was right. That mirror stuff works. When I was mad at Abby, the mirror showed me that I was really angry at myself, not her. Now Abby and I are friends again. I feel waaaay better after saying sorry. It's no fun fighting with people...

She dumped her stuff in the house and went straight out to the barn.

Sloshing through the backyard in her big black gum-boots, Zoey thought, what about all the other stuff Ama said... *I wonder if that works too? Yunno, the part about inner strength. What did she say again? Something about strong on the outside, gentle on the inside? No — the other way around. Oh yeah, I remember — the stronger you are on the inside, the gentler you can be on the outside.*

Huh? I still don't get it...

Zoey entered the calm, quiet oasis, brimming with an earthiness only piles of dirt, hay and horse manure could produce. As she peeked over Gypsy's stall door, Marble eyed her warily.

"You still afraid of me?" Zoey sighed. "Well, I guess I deserve it. I did scare you — *badly*. Sorry about that. I promise *never* to do that again. Will you *ever* forgive me?"

Marble perked her ears at the sound of Zoey's voice, then looked away, going back to nipping at her mom's flanks out of sheer boredom.

"I guess you don't believe what I say, though, do ya? Actions speak louder than words, right Marble? I'll leave ya alone to think about that — got chores to do now."

Pitchfork in hand, Zoey mucked stalls, filling wheelbarrow after wheelbarrow with golf ball-sized lumps of horse poop and pee-soaked sawdust mixed with leftover hay. She carefully tried to save as much of the good sawdust as possible, like her mom had shown her. After each wheelbarrow was full, she hauled it outside, through the gate and dumped it on the manure pile at the far side of the paddock. To avoid piles spreading out all over the paddock, she had to get her load on top of the manure pile rather than just dumping beside it. This meant balancing the wheelbarrow on a narrow board that acted as a kind of bridge, leading to the top of the pile. As she pushed a load

up, it slipped, catching her off guard and the weight of the thing sent her flying sideways into the muck, landing on her butt.

Yuck! I don't mind stepping in this stuff... but sitting in it? Ugh :~(No thanks!

She pulled herself up, wiped off as much poop as she could, then went back to work. *Thank goodness for gum-boots...and gloves...*

When she got to Gypsy's stall, she slowed down, moving deliberately around Marble. The filly watched her, but Zoey didn't try to pat her, or even look her in the eye.

"Thanks for pooping in one spot Gypsy. And you too Marble. Makes my job a whole lot easier. You horses are very neat and considerate, unlike cows." She rested on her pitchfork to make her point. "Cows don't care where they poop — all over the paddock! They'll even poop on their babies if they're in the way!" She scowled...then her face changed. "I like you guys much better — more discriminating, even if you do have a lot of it."

After all the stalls were mucked, Zoey decided to hang out in the barn awhile...

Maybe Marble'll warm up to me if I stay out here long enough... I'll just wait and let her come to me, rather than trying to go near her. I don't want a repeat of yesterday...

Crouching on her haunches along one edge of the stall, Zoey watched and waited. Five minutes later, Marble was looking at her, now with more curiosity than fear, but still not prepared to venture near. Boots sauntered over and curled up on some loose bits of hay beside Zoey's feet. Another ten minutes passed as Zoey stroked Boots's soft, black, white and brown fur. Marble still stood on the far side of the stall.

"Come on girl, it's just me," Zoey said, rocking from one leg to the other.

I wonder what everyone else is doing back at the house, she thought impatiently, starting to stand up. *Maybe I'll just forget this whole thing and try again another day.*

Then she remembered what Ama said: "Be calm, be patient — that's inner strength." *Okay, okay, I'll stay another ten minutes,* she conceded, looking at her watch.

Sitting down on the sawdust again, Zoey breathed in deeply to get rid of the itch she felt when she sat too long. Boots was purring loudly now, very content to be lying next to her. Zoey leaned back against the wall, letting her arms flop lazily by her side. Sensing her calm, Gypsy walked over and nuzzled her. Zoey closed her eyes, drinking in the attention from all the animals, leaving her worries behind.

* * *

Suddenly she was riding Marble bareback with no bridle, through a path in the forest, galloping freely as sunlight filtered through the tall pines... Marble's black mane and Zoey's dark hair were flying in the wind, intermingling with the sound of Marble's heavy breathing, Zoey laughing and the trees whispering... Marble responded instantly to the pressure of Zoey's legs, moving left and right in sync with her rider...

* * *

A tickling sensation on the back of her hand woke her up. Opening her eyes, she saw Marble's egg-shaped, velvety soft chin with whiskers poking out, resting on her hand.

Awww — she gasped. Looking up, she met Marble's brown eyes gazing back at her, only two feet away, as if the little foal was searching for what was inside her. Zoey felt a strange tingling sensation all over her body as a calm energy overwhelmed her and she noticed that the star on Marble's forehead seemed to glow.

The moment seemed to last forever, until —

"Clomp, clomp, clomp..."

Marble abruptly lifted up her head, backing away.

A rustling sound in the grain room...

Who's here?

Then a head poked up over the stall wall.

"Whatcha doing Zoey?"

"Just hangin out with the horses..." Zoey was a little annoyed that her peace had been disturbed. "What're you doing at home, mom?"

"Oh, I decided to head out early and spend some time at home tonight, for a change. Been working too much lately," she shook her head.

"Yeah, you can say that again," Zoey snickered under her breath.

"Well, maybe you can help me put these two out. Marble needs to get some fresh air before dinnertime. She's been stuck in this stall for the first few days of her life! Can you give me a hand leading one of them?"

"But mom, Marble's never had a halter on..."

"I know. First time for everything."

"But she might be afraid of it..." Zoey didn't want to tell her mom what had happened yesterday.

"Don't worry, she'll get over it. She can't stay in that stall forever, you know..." her mom shrugged her shoulders.

"Okay, I'll give it a shot..." Zoey said skeptically.

Zoey got the halter and lead rope from the grain room. The same ill-fated equipment she had used the day before. This time she didn't try to hide it from Marble, but entered the stall holding it out in front of her, for Marble to see in plain view.

Marble backed away at the sight of the rope.

"See, she's scared," Zoey said dejectedly.

"Just keep trying, don't give up so easily," her mom urged.

"Don't worry girl. It's just a halter. I won't put it on tight.

You're gonna have to trust me if you wanna go outside," Zoey called gently.

Zoey's mom put Gypsy's blue nylon halter on in three seconds flat and led her to the stall door. The old mare was a pro at this.

Bored of being cooped up in the barn, Marble stepped forward to sniff the leather halter. Zoey held still, letting Marble take her time.

"Zoey, we haven't got all day," her mom called.

"Hold on, gimme a minute".

Marble sniffed all parts of the halter and decided it wasn't so scary after all. She stood quietly beside her mother as Zoey calmly lifted it up, slid the bottom part over Marble's muzzle, the top piece behind her ears and fastened the metal buckle loosely.

"Good girl... good girl..." Zoey crowed. "See, it's not gonna hurt ya. Just a little piece of leather..."

I'm amazed Marble trusts me enough to let me put it on her, all without a fight, Zoey smiled. *Being calm and patient really works...*

Zoey's mom opened the stall door and walked Gypsy out. The mare stepped into the hallway. Marble wanted to follow, but whinnied nervously and stomped her feet, not budging. Gypsy looked back and nickered encouragingly, but Marble just threw her head up and down as if to say "come back, mom... come back!"

The filly's little hooves were rooted to the floor.

"Looks like she needs a little more encouragement than that," said Zoey's mom, walking Gypsy forward a few steps.

"Come on girl, just one foot in front of the other..." Zoey crooned. She stood next to Marble's head, then walked forward a step, gently tugging on the rope. Marble just stretched her neck out as her head was pulled forward, her hooves still planted.

"Stubborn little one, aren't ya?" For a split second Zoey considered pulling harder on the rope, but remembered Ama's words — 'strong on inside, gentle on outside'.

Instead of getting impatient and pulling harder, she relaxed the tension and stood next to Marble's head again.

"If you wanna go outside, you're gonna have to trust me. Your mom's going and I don't think you wanna be left behind. I know you've never been out before, but it's really cool out there." Zoey spoke in a firm tone while stroking the filly lovingly on the neck. "I'll wait for you if I have to, but I'm not backing down. We *are* going outside."

Sensing Zoey's steady determination, Marble perked her ears, then took one, small step forward.

"Good girl... you can do it." Zoey tugged gently at the halter, encouraging her forward again.

Another tentative step...

Suddenly, Marble snorted and leaped forward boldly, out of the stall and into the sunlit hallway.

"See, now that wasn't so bad, was it! I knew you could do it! You've got a big wide world to explore out there," Zoey grinned. "You're gonna love it, trust me."

Mare and foal walked out to their paddock together. Zoey and her mom released the lead ropes and watched Marble toss her head with delight at being free to roam outside. She reached down to sniff a flower budding up from the ground, then flared her nostrils, spun around and cantered off to explore another part of the paddock.

"I think she trusts you Zoey. Not easy to get a foal to lead like that first time round."

"Yeah, well, it took some time. I've never been so patient in my life...been out here a couple hours..." she said, smiling at Marble over the cedar fence..."and it feels good."

That little horse's definitely worth it.

She was surprised by the warm, relaxed feeling throughout her whole body.

And so am I...

10

Not Again!

"Zoey, come get pancakes with strawberries and whipped cream!" her mom called from the kitchen, the next morning.

"Yummo! I'm there!" replied Zoey enthusiastically, bounding downstairs on the sunny saturday.

"Here ya go, sweetie," her mom said, piling Zoey's plate high with fluffy golden treats. A dollop of thick, white whipped cream sat on top, slathered with bright red strawberries covered with sauce...

"Um-hmm... DELICIOSO!" cried Zoey in sheer delight.

Tucking into her yummy breakfast, she couldn't help think what a great day this was turning out to be already...

Everything's going so well for me since I blew out all my frustrations on the punching bag the other day... Ama taught me some cool stuff, I made up with Abby, taught Marble how to lead and now mom made my favorite breakfast — how awesome is that?!

After mopping up every bit of strawberry sauce with the

last morsels of pancake, she dumped her plate in the sink and sashayed around the kitchen, ipod in her ears, rocking to her fav tunes.

"Thanks mom, that was amazingly… SCRUMPDOODLELICIOUS!"

"No sweat, my dear. Now I need a little help from you though. Can you vacuum the side door before you go out to the barn?"

"Sure thing!"

She grabbed the old vacuum out of the closet and plugged it in. As the machine head rolled back and forth between black gum-boots, worn sneakers, high heels, flat black karate slippers, white super-padded snow-boots and plain leather shoes, Zoey cranked up her music and hummed along, as if all the dirt inside her were being sucked out too.

Unplugging the machine, she shouted, "I'm done! Going outside now. See ya later."

"Thanks kiddo," her mom answered, but Zoey was already out the door.

On the way to the barn, she noticed the signs of spring around her.

Cool… all the snow has melted in the last couple days — it's really warmed up now. Look at that crocus bud popping out of the grass… and the robins are singing…

Bear came jogging over, wagging his tail.

Even ol' Bear's more energetic than usual…

"Beautiful day, eh Bear?!" She ran her hand across his furry back.

"Race ya to the barn… ready, set go!" Zoey took off at a sprint, with Bear close behind. He caught up as they neared the building, nearly bowling her over with his burly chest.

Zoey slid the door open. "Good morning you guys!" she called to all the horses.

Excited nickers and stomping hooves greeted her.

"Breakfast time!"

An hour later, the horses were fed and watered and their stalls cleaned.

Zoey got ready to lead Marble outside.

"You ready to explore the world again?"

Marble nickered and pushed her nose into Zoey's face.

"I'll take that as a YES…"

Walking beside the filly, leading her to the paddock, Zoey spotted something on the gravel path. *That's funny, I didn't see anything here when I first came out… I wonder what that is?*

Just then, the sound of laughter caught her ear. She looked up and caught a glimpse of Kev racing out their driveway on his bike, with Jake and Ryan in tow.

Huh? That's weird. Kev's never been to my place before. And I didn't invite him… haven't really thought about him since we got into that fight the other day. I just avoid him at school and he avoids me… suits me just fine… I guess he's visiting Jake coz Kev

doesn't live in Cablecar... I wonder what they're doin' here?
KA-BOOM!

Her thoughts were cut short by a loud crackling explosion. Marble reared up in alarm, startled by the violent noise, yanking Zoey's arm with surprising strength for a young foal.

BANG!
CRACK!
POP!

"OUCH!!" Zoey yelled, as Marble landed on her right foot. Zoey grabbed her toe, hopping on the other leg as Marble took off at a gallop, snorting in terror, lead rope trailing dangerously behind her on the ground.

Watching the filly helplessly and wincing in pain, Zoey called out, "slow down girl, you're gonna get hurt!" But Marble just continued at full speed, past the dark green horse trailer, around the equipment shed and down the full-length of the riding ring.

Looking back toward the driveway, Zoey's mind whirled...

Marble's faster than me, but Kev's not. I could grab my bike and chase after him... Boy, am I gonna KILL him when I catch him! Not just for what he did to me, but for Marble! He really made me FURIOUS this time...

She turned toward the garage to run and grab her bike, then suddenly changed her mind.

Wait a sec. Breathe. Just calm down Zoey. What about Marble? You just gonna leave her out like that? Lead rope dangling down, outside her paddock. STOP! Take care of your horse first. You can deal with Kev later...

Zoey put her sore foot down gingerly.

But Marble's terrified. She's not gonna let me catch her if she senses my anger. I've gotta calm down first. Take three deep breaths girl...

Zoey raised her arms, palms out in front of her, as if slowing the world down.

ONE...

She took a deep inhale, felt fresh air enter her nose and lungs, linger there for a moment, then come whooshing out her mouth...

TWO...

She counted to three breathing in, with five counts breathing out. An eternity, it seemed... until she could actually feel the rage inside her go down...

THREE...

Now concentrating more on the feeling of her breath than how angry she was, Zoey felt a wave of calm wash over her...

She walked around the equipment shed to see Marble standing at the edge of the pine forest. The filly obviously wanted to be as far away as possible from that terrifying noise, without going into the woods. Zoey approached her very slowly. Marble's chest was heaving, her eyes still wide with terror.

"It's okay Marble... it's just me," Zoey reassured her. "Those boys are gone. That firecracker's done. It's just you and me now."

As she uttered the words 'those boys', Zoey felt herself tense up again...

Just breath Zoey, stay calm... BREATHE...

Forcing herself to take deep inhalations and exhalations with every step, Zoey eventually got close to Marble. Holding her halter, she stroked the foal's neck in long, gentle sweeps, talking to her in a slow, deep voice. "Hey girl, everything's okay... I'm here now... I'm gonna take care of you."

Sweaty and shaking, Marble looked at Zoey, gently nudging her. Zoey felt something on her hand and when she looked down, saw that it was red.

Is that what I think it is?

Blood dripped down her palm.

"Oh no!" Zoey recoiled, horror-struck.

A deep gash ran down Marble's face.

"You're hurt!" she gasped. "Pretty bad — come on, let's get you back to the barn and fix you up."

Marble resisted walking at first, then reluctantly followed, but struggled to keep up.

"You're limping too?!" Zoey groaned.

Marble couldn't put weight on her right hind leg.

"Is Kev ever gonna DIE for this..." Heat rose in her again as she thought of his dangerous, downright stupid prank.

Not now Zoey... Breathe... remember?

Just take three deep breaths...

One...

She sucked in a big gulp of air...

Two...

Another big inhale and even longer exhale...
Three...
She opened up her lungs until they could expand no more, then slowly released as much air as she possibly could...
That's better. Stay calm. For Marble's sake.
Back in the stall, Zoey washed Marble's cut with antiseptic solution. She didn't know what to do about her leg. *I think I'd better go tell someone...*

In the house, she ran into her grandma.
"Hi Zoey, what you doing?"
"Hey Ama, I was outside," she said breathlessly, "Marble got hurt coz some boys from school set off a firecracker in our yard!"
"Oh—no! She okay?"
"She ran away from me and cut herself on the face, plus her leg's all weird! I think we need to call the vet..."
"AIEYAAHHH!...Why those boys do that?"
"I'm gonna *kill* Kev," Zoey said, narrowing her eyes. "Is he ever gonna get it for pulling this prank. I'm soooo mad at him, I could just hang him up by his toenails..."
"Zoey," Ama said seriously, "you always have choice. No matter what someone do to you, you always have **CHOICE** how to react."
"Huh?!" Zoey squawked. *What's she talking about now?!*
"What do you mean Ama?" she sighed, regaining her

composure.

"You can be angry, get him back, but then what happen? You feel better? Maybe for short time, but then he get you back. Bad feeling never end. You want to be angry your whole life?" She scrunched her wizened face so it looked like a saggy elephant butt...

"What's the other choice, Ama?" Zoey challenged her.

Ama paused, then lowered her voice and whispered — ,

" — you can show love."

Zoey nearly doubled over, laughing.

"WHAT?!

  LOVE?

    FOR WHAT HE DID?

      YOU MUST BE KARAAZEEEE!"

"No Zoey, not crazy. That is truth. Not easy. But truth."

"Whoa, Ama, that's way too tall an order for me. Nope, there's no waaaay I can show love after the stunt he just pulled."

"Everyone need love Zoey. *Especially* when they not deserve it," Ama said firmly, standing her ground despite Zoey's theatrical response. *"Show love* not mean you do nice thing for him. It mean you first show love for yourself."

Settling down enough to talk normally, Zoey asked, "how do I do that?"

"Have inner strength — calm, patient, firm, trust."

Oh no, not that inner strength stuff again, Zoey groaned silently... *But hey, it did work with Marble, leading her out of the stall that first time. Maybe I should listen...*

"Don't do anything to him. Not fight. Not mean thing. Not nice thing. Just ignore, as if it not happen. But inside, you strong...you love yourself. He will feel it," Ama said, pounding her heart with her hand for emphasis.

"You mean, **actions speak louder than words?** Don't say anything? Don't do anything?

"Yes. You not do anything. Not evil eye either, okay?"

"But won't he think I'm just too chicken to get back at him?"

"No. You not give CHICKEN ENERGY — "

" — you give strong energy. LOVE ENERGY. It look the same on outside, but on inside feel very different. He will know. He feel your energy more than he hear your words."

"Hmmph..." Zoey scratched her head and looked sideways at Ama.

What planet are you on Ama?! On earth we use words and actions to say what we mean, not this invisible energy stuff...

"Only Zoey choose how to respond, okay? Not let anyone else control you by their actions... by what they do to you." Ama peered deep into Zoey's eyes to see if she really got it.

Zoey looked away, breaking off Ama's stare, lost in thought... Then she looked down at her feet and shook her head.

"Nope. Sorry, Ama. Can't do it. I can't make that choice. Kev doesn't deserve it."

"You not do it for Kev," Ama said, surprised. "You do it for yourself. **Anger hurt you much more than it hurt anyone else.**" Then she turned away, knowing Zoey was no longer listening.

Stunned and confused, Zoey had forgotten how much her foot hurt. Now that the conversation was over, she felt it throbbing again. It reminded her of how angry she was...

I've got to get this fire outta me, she realized, running upstairs, kicking open her bedroom door and punching her pillow. *I'd better go to the basement before I bust something...*

She launched herself onto the punching bag, hitting it as hard as she possibly could. Spastic anger poured out of her as her arms flailed on the leather. Loud grunts and growls escaped from her with each attack.

After awhile, she couldn't keep up the intensity. As her angered lessened, her punches became more refined, until they were powerful, synchronized movements involving her whole body. Every few punches, she let out a KIAI! as loud as she could, releasing any lingering pent up frustration onto the bag.

Over a hundred punches later, she dropped her arms, completely spent, sucking wind... Feeling better, but still not sure what to do about Kev, Zoey headed back out to the barn to check on Marble. As she climbed the stairs, she thought of Ama's words — "have inner strength..."

Hah, I'll show strength — outer strength. I'll punch him out.

Later that day Marble stood head down in her stall, but perked her ears when Zoey walked in. Limping over, she nuzzled Zoey with her soft cheek as if to say "got any treats for me?"

"Oh Marble, you're such an amazing horse. Even when you're hurt, you're still so loving... so trusting. You forgive me for that halter ruckus we went through, don't you?" Zoey rubbed her forelock. "You've been with us less than a week, but I don't know what I'd do without you..."

Just then it started to pour...

Zoey listened to the sound of raindrops hitting the metal roof. A slow patter at first, then a faster drum beat, until the rain pounded down like a symphony. Wrapping her arms around the little foal, Zoey felt her heart beat against Marble's chest.

The foal's heartbeat was slower than her own. Zoey breathed deeply and the rhythm of her heart slowed until it matched Marble's. They stood in silence for what seemed like an hour — two hearts beating as one...

In the stillness, it hit her.

Marble forgave me and trusted me again after my mistake.

She's even loving NOW, after the firecracker scare. She doesn't know who put it there — coulda been me for all she knows. Yet she trusts me again. Wow, this little horse is like a BOOMERANG... always returning to love.

"Well, you're way more hurt than me. If you can do it, so can I," Zoey said with a glint in her eye. Kissing Marble on her wet nose, she lay her face against the filly's soft furry cheek.

"I"m not exactly sure what to do, but I'll try. Or maybe it's what *not* to do. What did Ama say? 'Don't do anything, just be strong inside.' "

Over the next few days, Zoey kept to herself at school, focusing her energy on her work and on staying calm. Each time she saw Kev, Jake or Ryan, she reminded herself to take a deep breath. While the air was going out of her lungs, she'd repeat to herself *"no one can make me do or feel anything. **I choose how I react**.*"

She could feel Kev watching her, expecting her to lash out at him, throw a fit, or do *something*. When she didn't, he was shocked — puzzled at first, then he started to feel bad.

A few days later Kev walked over to her in science class while she was sorting different sized frogs for her science fair experiment.

"Hey Zoey," he said casually, looking around.

"Hi," she replied curtly, not turning to look at him.

"Uh...uh...how's Marble?" he asked tentatively, wringing his hands together and peering over her shoulder.

"Why? Who wants to know?" she turned around and lifted her science goggles onto her forehead as her orange bangs flashed in the light. She was barely able to contain herself now that he was bringing all that up again.

"Whoa, I just wanna know if she's okay... I know she got hurt the other day when we pulled that stunt at your place," he said sheepishly.

"Yeah, she did, so what's it to you?" Zoey crossed her arms.

"Hey, I just wanna say sorry. I didn't mean to hurt your horse. Just wanted to get you back for humiliating me in the fight last week," he blurted out, looking like a sad, lost puppy.

"She coulda broken her leg yunno. Then we woulda had to put her down," Zoey replied sternly, folding her arms down by her side.

"Yeah, I heard you had to call the vet. But she's okay, right?"

"She'll be fine, just a cut on her nose and a sprained leg... But you didn't have to take it out on my horse. She didn't do anything to you."

"I wasn't planning to. I didn't know you were gonna lead her outta the barn just then. Well...like I said, I'm sorry Zoey..."

Zoey remained silent, staring through his eyes to see if

he really was sorry, or if he was just saying stuff.

"Hmmph — okay." On the one hand she was pleasantly surprised he had apologized.

But on the other hand, words were not enough.

11

Romance in the Air...

A couple months went by... the fight and firecracker incidents gradually faded to the back of Zoey's memory. Her life was full up with karate practice, piano lessons, homework, chores, horseback riding and trying out new pastries from Jill's Bake Shop. And keeping her little brother Zack off her back.

She barely even had time to hang with Abby! Except at school, that was... But there was one thing that began to take up more and more space in her mind. There was a buzz going around the school about it. Everyone was talking about what they'd wear and gossiping over who would go with who, to... the dance.

Zoey wasn't a clothes horse by any stretch of the imagination, but she wasn't so completely without sense that she would go in her barn clothes either. So *'what to wear to the dance'* did cross her mind. Most of the girls in her class wanted to be asked out by Kev or one of his friends to the social event of the year...

In the hallway, just about to head to gym class, she heard something…

"Uh, hey, Zoey…"

"Yeah," She spun around to see who was talking to her.

Kev stood alone, his feet shifting nervously on the beige vinyl floor, his eyes darting everywhere but at her.

What's up with him?! Zoey wondered. Got ants in his pants? He looks like someone who's about to tell a fib. Speaking of which, what's the big deal about lying anyway? mom and dad are always telling me: 'whatever you do, don't lie to me. You won't get in trouble if you tell the truth.' I haven't decided whether I believe them or not...

"Uh... uh... sorry, I gotta go..." Kev pressed his fingers together like a spider doing pushups on a mirror... then turned and started walking quickly the other way.

Zoey watched him for a moment, then moved toward the stairs...

That's weird? Oh, who cares anyhow...

What was I on about... Oh yeah, fibbing — adults don't lie, do they? Yeah, uh-huh...They just call it something else. Funny words like sarcasm, storytelling, or 'half-truths'. Sometimes they lie with their actions but not their words — like the time I caught mom smoking a cigarette in the bathroom after everyone was asleep. We all thought she had sworn off cigarettes months earlier. Is that better or worse than lying with words? I figure it's worse, coz more muscles are involved. Anytime you do an action with your body, lots of muscles move. But when you talk it's just your mouth moving. Unless you smile of course. That actually involves moving seventeen muscles in your face. Yeah, just to smile? Can you believe it?! Didn't know it was that complicated to look happy did ya? Did you even know you had that many muscles in your face? Frowning though? That involves twenty-six muscles! So there you go. It's easier to look happy than mad.

Just about to go down the stairs, she heard heavy breathing behind her as if someone had run to catch up. She glanced over her shoulder at the person, now beside her. Baffled, she turned to look at him.

"Wassup Kev?"

This time he didn't wait till his nerves got the better of him.

"Uh... uh... you w-wanna go to the dance with me?" he sputtered awkwardly.

Zoey's jaw dropped.

Her eyes and mouth popped open as if someone had just pulled a wedgie on her. The voice in her head had a field day...

I can't believe my ears! I thought he hated my guts since I showed him up in front of all his friends, not to mention the whole school. I haven't really thought twice about him since he

apologized for that stunt he pulled with the firecracker... besides, I don't really like boys in general...

"Well, you gonna give me an answer?" he asked.

Zoey stared down at her feet, feeling extremely

embarrassed...

Caught completely off guard, she didn't have time for a measured response. She looked up at him, abruptly shouted "NO!," then turned and ran down the stairs, into the girls changing room.

Kev was so stunned, he just stood immobile for a minute, a confused look on his face. He was standing in the exact same spot where he'd ridiculed Zoey a couple months earlier.

She avoided him at school the rest of the day and couldn't wait to get home.

After walking home from the bus stop, she headed for the comfort of her room, curling up on her carpet and staring at the ceiling, trying to make sense of the day's events.

A few minutes later the front door open. "Zoey, can you help me with these groceries," her dad called before ducking outside to get another load.

"What about my sisters?!" she shouted in reply. "Can't you ask them? I'm busy!"

Can't a girl have a few moments of peace around here?! I just wanna be left alone... unloading groceries is the last thing I need...

Silence.

Then the rustling sound of plastic bags and the click-click of shoes on the hardwood floor.

"Phew" she thought to herself, "got out of that one. I just

don't feel like doing anything right now."

"Zoey! Get down here right now, I need your help!" She could hear the annoyed tone in her dad's voice.

"Yeah, OK, I'm coming," she grumbled. With a sigh, she pulled herself up off the floor and marched downstairs.

They worked in silence, hauling bags of groceries inside, unloading them onto the kitchen floor, then sorting everything into its place — veggies and fruit in the bottom compartments of the fridge, cereal and cookies in the corner cupboard, cleaning supplies and potatoes under the sink.

You'd think a whole army lived in our house with the amount of food dad bought...

The job almost done, dad looked much happier and broke the silence.

"I saw Abby's mom at the store today. She said there's a school dance coming up next week. You planning on going?"

Wedging cereal boxes into the cupboard, making sure her favorite was at the back, out of view of her ravenous siblings, Zoey paused a moment, wondering whether she should tell her dad about Kev asking her out.

"Uh, I don't know yet... depends what Abby wants to do..." she replied.

Her dad didn't buy it. "Since when have you been so laid back about going to a dance? You were sooo upset last year when you had to come back early because your sister started puking on the dance floor. You surprised yourself with how much fun you had, didn't you?"

"Well, things change..."

Zoey's dad scrunched up all the shopping bags and shoved them under the sink.

"Oh, guess who I ran into the other day at the car repair shop?"

"I dunno," Zoey shrugged her shoulders.

"The father of that boy you got into a fight with a while ago. What's his name — ?"

" — Kev…his name's Kev," she interrupted. "Why would the dance have anything to do with him?" she slipped up.

Her dad raised his eyebrows. "Ohhhhh. You don't mention many boy's names around this house. He's the only one who came to mind... what were the words his dad used?" Zoey's dad scratched his head, trying to remember. "Oh yeah... *'your daughter sure made an impression on my son'*. That's what he said to me."

"That was months ago dad and it wasn't exactly like we were friends. We got into a fight, remember?"

"I know, I know, but sometimes strong emotions go both ways — he apologized later, right?"

"Wow, you're like a detective, grilling me with questions..." she frowned. "Yeah, it does have to do with him... he asked me if I want to go to the dance with him and I was so surprised, I shouted NO!"

Her dad paused a moment. Out of the corner of her eye, Zoey could see him chuckling to himself.

What's so funny about that? He doesn't have to make fun of me…

Just as she was about to protest her dad's reaction out loud, he responded.

"I know you don't really like him because of what he did to you, but maybe you could've been a bit softer on him? Grade seven boys do have *ego's* you know." Zoey's dad looked up absently, as if remembering something from his own childhood. Then he pulled a large chicken out of a bag and plopped it onto the chopping board.

"What's an 'eh-go'?" Zoey asked.

"EEE-go, not eh-go."

"Okay, whatever. What's an EEE-go?"

"It's the most fragile part of us. The part that you can't see — that makes us feel separate from everyone else. Our ego tries to puff ourselves up so we feel big and powerful, or shrink ourselves so we feel tiny and inferior. Sometimes we do stupid things because of our ego."

"You mean, like calling people names, totally unprovoked?" Zoey offered.

"Something like that" he replied.

BANG! The butcher knife in his hand came crashing down on a piece of chicken thigh, cracking it in two.

A thought popped into Zoey's head as she remembered

the conversation with Ama a couple months back.

"If your ego helps you feel powerful, is it the same as 'inner strength'?" she asked.

"Ha-ha. No, not quite." Her dad put the knife down and washed his hands in the sink. "Come and sit down with me Zoey," he gestured to the wooden chairs tucked under the dining table.

"There's a *BIG* difference between ego and inner strength" her dad explained. "*Inner strength* is developing power inside you — power over *yourself*. The ability to control your own emotions, feel good about yourself, not be bothered by what others say or do to you, even if its unkind — the ability to stand up for what you believe in. Inner strength has to do with you alone, not with anyone else. Only you can build it for yourself."

"Okay...." Zoey said slowly, "I get it, like when I stood up to Kev for calling me names."

"That's right."

"Ego, on the other hand, is about power over *others*," he continued. "The ego is always trying to get you to feel either better than or worse than everyone else." Her dad tore another piece of chicken from the bone.

When you feel better than others, you might do or say things to make others feel smaller and yourself even bigger. When Kev called you names at school he might have done it to boost his own ego and feel a stronger sense of belonging with his friends. If you had cowered and appeared scared when Kev called you names, that would probably have boosted his ego."

"But when I beat him in the fight his ego shrunk instead?"

"You got it."

"Losing a fight to a girl was probably a big blow to his ego. I'm sure it took him awhile to get over it. We all have egos. There's nothing wrong with them until they take over and we start doing mean things to others just to make ourselves feel good. Ironically, a person with a big ego usually doesn't have a lot of inner strength... they need to *appear* better than others, precisely because they *feel* inferior," Her dad finished, got up from his chair and headed to the fridge to start making dinner.

"OK, let's get back to the point," her dad announced, rinsing chicken juice from his hands, then pulling vegetables from the fridge and placing them on the chopping board. "Kev asked you to the dance, which probably took a lot of courage on his part, especially since you beat him up a few months ago and that hurt his ego. You shouted 'NO!' and ran away... Why'd you say no?"

"Uh, I dunno... i guess I'm still a little mad at him for calling me names and for hurting Marble. He sorta weirded me out with that question."

"Hurting Marble was an accident. Didn't he apologize for that already?"

"Yeah, well... I don't like boys anyway. And I'm not sure I even wanna go to the dance..."

Her dad just looked at her, remaining silent.

"Okay, so maybe I'm still mad at him. He never apologized for calling me names."

"Did you apologize for humiliating him in that fight?"

"No."

"You gonna stay mad at him forever?"

"No."

"Does being mad make you feel good?"

"No."

"Remember, it's your CHOICE how you feel Zoey, not his. You can *choose* to forgive, or choose to stay mad. Up to you. Put yourself in his shoes for a minute and think about how he might feel." He glanced up from chopping celery to see Zoey's reaction.

"Hmm, well, he probably doesn't feel great. In fact, he probably feels pretty lousy. Maybe a little embarrassed, a little hurt and hey, even angry. That's how I'd feel if I extended my hand to someone and they used it to slap me in the face."

OHMAGOSH!! Did I really do that? she cried to herself.

Pausing to think for a minute, her surprise gradually turned to righteousness. "Well…serves him right. That's exactly what he did to me."

"Two wrongs don't make a right Zoey," Her dad

gave her a kind but firm look. It was the same look he had when he called us to do chores — like we'd better listen, because he meant business.

"Maybe... but the truth is I don't want to go to the dance with him, unless of course he really is sorry for what he did."

"Well maybe you should tell him how what *he* did made *you* feel," her dad suggested, handing Zoey a piece of celery to munch on. "Maybe you should give him a second chance?"

"Yeah…I could," she said slowly, carefully turning the idea over in her head like a rotisserie chicken.

"Thanks dad, I'll think about it..."

Zoey saw Kev in the school hallway the next day. He was walking alone this time. She considered marching right past him and forgetting about what she and her dad talked about, but her intuition overtook her.

"You know, you really hurt my feelings when you called me names before," she blurted out before she could stop herself. Looking down at her running shoes, she felt embarrassed to be expressing her feelings to a boy like this, leaving herself vulnerable. But she thought back to what her dad said: 'tell him how what *he* did made *you* feel and give him a second chance.' She also remembered what Ama told her on the day of the fight and knew more was expected of her because she studied karate. "Have some inner strength Zoey," she thought to herself, *inner strength*.

"Called you names? What? That was months ago," Kev replied in shock.

Great... maybe I shouldn't have said anything... now he's gonna think that's all I've been thinking about for the past couple months...

Kev cast his eyes down, slumping his shoulders so his backpack almost fell off, his hair falling across his face. "I'm sorry. I didn't mean to hurt your feelings. I just... just wanted to look cool in front of my friends," he explained.

"You don't have to make someone feel bad in order for you to feel good," she replied, looking him straight in the eye.

He looked up. "Yeah and you don't have to humiliate people in a fight either..."

"Hey, I'm sorry about that. I guess I get a little crazy when I get punched in the face. Can't control myself, yunno...," Zoey shrugged with a little laugh.

"Well I guess we both have to try a little harder then... sometimes I hear this little voice in my head telling me what I *should* do, but it doesn't jive with what I *want* to do," Kev admitted.

"Yeah, I know. It's like there are these two voices in my head. The good voice — that's my INTUITION. It's hard, but we should listen to our intuition a little more often. If you follow it, you won't go wrong."

"INTUITION? Where'd you learn about that?" Kev looked surprised.

"Karate class. How do you think I knew which way you were going to move when we had it out behind the parking lot a couple months ago? It wasn't a fluke. I was watching your eyes and listening to that little voice inside me, my *intuition*."

Nodding his head, Kev took a deep breath and looked up at Zoey.

"That's cool. I'll give it a shot. Anyway, I sure learned my lesson about calling *you* names," he grinned.

Smiling, Zoey started to walk away...

He really is sorry for what he did... Well, I guess I could forgive him then...And he did have the nerve to put his ego behind him and ask me in the first place...That probably required some inner strength on his part — to go to the dance with someone who punched him out...

She turned around and looked back at Kev standing by himself in the hallway, his yellow t-shirt and green sneakers sticking out against the beige floor tile. Somehow he looked much more relaxed without all his friends around. Stripped of his role of most popular boy in the school, leader of the 'tough grade seven boys', Zoey saw that he was just another kid, with all the same fears as everyone else.

She called out, "Oh, by the way, I guess I will go to the dance with you... if you still want to. You're not so bad, after all."

12

B.E.W.C.

Zoey and her mom drove to the only mall in town to pick out a dress for the dance. Walking through the bright, noisy atrium, she wondered if the dance was worth it — worth shopping for, that was.

I don't like shopping. I mean, it's fun for about twenty minutes, but gets old real fast if you don't find something you like. Pulling clothes on and off, undoing my belt and taking off my shoes a million times just to try on lots of different stuff that may or may not look good. I'm not that great at coordinating clothes and end up buying stuff that feels comfortable, even if it doesn't look super. I hardly ever buy the latest fashions unless it's grungy or plain ol' casual and can hardly remember the last time I wore a skirt or a dress. I get tired just thinking about going through the racks for something I might like...

Fifty minutes later, she hit the wall.

"Mom, can we just go home? I think I'll borrow something

from one of my sisters.   Between the two of them there's gotta be a dress that'll look good on me."

Hunting through her older sister's closet, she found it. A cute, shiny, brown dress with silver asian flowers, a V-neck and a sash to tie around her waist.

Just my style. Not too fancy, not too plain. I've got some brown flats with a small bow on top that'll go perfectly with it. That's as frilly as I get... And brown's good — I wouldn't dream of wearing pink...

Holding the dress up against her body, staring at herself in the mirror, Zoey studied the face she saw in front of her.

Hmm, a couple zits on my forehead. Oh well, no one will see them coz they're on my hairline.

Her dark hair was cut in layers framing her oval face. Even the orange bit didn't stick out so bad. But thick, unplucked eyebrows fanned out from above her smooth nose, which carried a slight indent on the ridge of skin between her two nostrils (a trademark from her Scottish side). Small, unpierced ears with virtually no lobe lay flat against her head.

Almost all my friends have their ears pierced, but I never really saw the point. Just one more piece of jewelry I'd have to take off each time I have a karate workout. No jewelry's allowed during training because with one punch, it could become permanently embedded on you — a 'karate piercing', Zoey laughed.

She grabbed her earlobe and pulled it down to see how far it would stretch.

The upside of wearing earrings doesn't seem worth it — dangly pieces of colored metal hanging from my ears to make me look better? Reminds me of the National Geographic special I saw about an African tribe where the women wore rings around their necks to elongate them. Long, giraffe-like necks were seen as beautiful in their culture. More rings meant more beauty. Weird how each culture has their own idea of what beauty is...

She held a pair of big silver hoops up to her ears...

That tribe might look at us wearing earrings and think it's just as funny looking. So if I don't think earrings are worth the trouble, why bother?

Continuing her facial scan, she noticed the medium full lips covering her buck teeth.

"Thank goodness my lips aren't thin, or they'd never cover my teeth!"

All in all, not a bad picture for a girl, she smiled. *I could look better with a little makeup on, if only I knew how to do that. But I'm not desperate enough to go to the trouble of figuring make-up out. Besides, I don't have any...*

She pulled her hair back into a ponytail, then let it down again.

I'm always wearing it up for karate... maybe I'll just leave it down for once. My glasses look a bit geekish, but hey — I gotta see...

As she held the dress up against her body and looked in the mirror, she noticed that the flower pattern on the dress made her look taller than normal. "Niiiiice," she said aloud, taking a spin around, "this will do just fine."

"Mom, can you hurry up? Pleeease!" Zoey yelled.
"Just a second...gotta find the car keys!" her mom shouted from the down the hall. "They're missing from the bowl... again! Arrrrgh!"

As they drove into town, past mountains and endless swaths of evergreen trees, Zoey sat quietly, wondering what tonight's dance would be like. The dark northern night felt like a cloak around her. No one could see her, or tell what was going on in her head. Finally, her mom broke the silence.

"You're awfully quiet Zoey. What's on your mind?"

"Oh nothing…" she hesitated. Then continued slowly, "just a little nervous about tonight."

"Nervous, why?"

"You know…going to the dance with Kev 'n all. It's not like I've done that before. I'm not quite sure what I'm supposed to do."

"Hmm, good point," her mom paused, staring over the steering wheel at the road ahead.

A few moments passed in silence.

"Why not just be yourself and have fun?" her mom added matter-of-factly, glancing at Zoey with a smile.

"Yeah, easier said than done," Zoey mumbled under her breath.

"Are you sure you don't want me to come inside with you?" Zoey's mom dropped her off at the main door of the school.

"No, I'll be fine mom, don't worry," Zoey rolled her eyes.

"I'll be here to pick you up at ten o'clock."

"Okay, see you," Zoey jumped out of the car, cast one last backward glance at the familiar red tail-lights of the family bus, then pivoted around and dashed inside the school. A steady stream of kids entered with her. Looking around, she spotted a familiar face.

"Hey Abby," she called out above the sound of car engines, chatter and music.

Abby didn't hear her.

"ABBY!" she yelled, cupping her hands over her mouth.

"Oh, hi Zoey," Abby said, turning around to greet her. The two friends gave each other a hug even though it had only been a few hours since they saw each other. Glad to have company, their nerves faded to excitement as they checked in their coats.

"Wanna go in?" Abby asked, pointing to the gym doors.

"Sure, why not." Zoey tried to sound much more cool, calm and collected than she felt.

Stepping into the dance hall, they were both stunned

at the transformation. It looked nothing like it did during P.E. class earlier the same day. Cloaked in darkness, with multi-colored beams of light swirling around the vast room and a red velvet cloth covering the front of the stage, their exercise haven had become a mysteriously enchanting dance hall. A peach-colored sign saying "*Eagle Elementary End of Year Dance*" greeted everyone as they entered. Glittering streamers adorned the walls where exercise posters had lain before. A DJ bopped to top forty hits behind stacks of black gadgety sound equipment on the stage.

Some kids were dancing to the rocking music in the center of the gym while others hung back along the gym walls, not yet ready to join the fray. The hall was far from full, as people were still arriving. Abby and Zoey spotted a group of friends and walked over to join them by the far end of the gym. Somehow she felt more motivated to join the group now than ever before. Normally, she and Abby liked to hang by themselves and do their own thing. But tonight, in an unfamiliar setting, there was a feeling of safety in numbers.

Am I ever glad I've got friends, she thought to herself, glancing at the lone kid standing next to their group.

Surveying the dance floor, surrounded by her friends, Zoey started to loosen up and feel more at ease. 'Just be yourself and have fun', she remembered her mom saying in the car.

I think I can do that...

Suddenly a hush came over her group of friends. Kev, Jake and Ryan approached.

"Hey Zoey."

"Hi Kev". She was a little embarrassed to be having this conversation in front of her entire group of friends.

"I was waiting for you outside, but you must've come in before me," He surprised her with his honesty.

"Oh yeah, I came in with Abby," she replied casually.

Zoey felt the curious eyes of everyone in the group on her. They all knew what had happened between them a couple months earlier behind the parking lot. She felt the tension build as she and Kev both looked down, wondering what to say next.

Weird to be standing here at the dance with the same guy I did 'double up' on a few months back, winding him so badly he couldn't stand up...

Kev glanced up.

"Well, you wanna dance?" he asked, with a sudden surge of confidence.

"Yeah, sure". With a broad grin across her face, she took his outstretched hand and walked out to the middle of the dance floor.

Moving her feet to the beat, swinging her arms, her hair flopping loosely around her face, Zoey gradually got lost in the music, forgetting about the eyes on her. Pretty soon a bunch of friends joined them and they all danced together in a circle, smiling and laughing at each other.

This feels good. Really good. I'm happy, without a care in the world right now...

A few songs later, she and Kev took a break at the water fountain.

"You're alright," she said. "I guess there are other sides to you I didn't see before."

"You thought I was just a dumb, mean jock, didn't you?" he laughed.

"Well... no... not exactly. Uh... okay... yeah... so what if I did?" she smiled. "You thought I was just a nerdy karate kid, didn't you?"

"Yeah, sorta..."

"Well, I guess there's more to each of us then... We shouldn't be so quick to judge!"

"Yeah, at least not till you've danced with the other person!" he chuckled.

A catchy beat started booming from the speakers.

"Come on, let's get back out there, I love this song!"

That night, after coming home from the dance, Zoey lay awake in bed, processing the days events. Her body still tingled from the excitement of the dance and her mind churned like an ice-cream maker. She was nowhere near going to sleep...

I haven't had this much fun in ages...

She looked out the window at the clear sky speckled with stars and a grin slid across her face.

And I didn't even wear make-up, or earrings. Hah! Maybe that's why I feel so good — I did what I wanted and didn't worry about what others thought of me...

Hmm, maybe that's what Kev likes about me — strong on the inside. More importantly, that's what I'm beginning to like about myself...

All of a sudden the question Ama asked months earlier popped into her head.

"What does inner strength mean to you Zoey?"

She felt a swirl of emotion inside her — lots of different feelings all mixed together to form a big mess. She'd been on a roller coaster of emotions these past couple months.

As she looked up at the scattered stars outside her window, she saw a pattern emerge out of the chaos and all of a sudden the letters of her name appeared — Z L — brilliant and bold in the night sky.

Then it hit her.

I get it! It's just the same with inner strength — there's a pattern to all these emotions I'm feeling. It's actually really simple...

Inner strength is easy to spot once you learn to see it, just like my initials amongst the stars . It always feels good in my gut — like I know what I'm doing is right, even if it's not that easy. That feeling is my guiding light, just like a bright star.

— It's that calm, firm, trust I had when I first led Marble out of her stall (it felt good to be patient).

— It's recognizing that when I'm mad at someone else, I'm really mad at myself... like when I was angry at Abby (it felt good to apologize for blowing up at her).

— It's choosing to forgive someone even when they do something that hurts me... like when Kev set off that firecracker (it felt good to forgive Kev).

— And most of all, it's choosing to breathe deeply, release my pain in a positive way and react with calm confidence even when everything seems to be falling apart (it felt good to let loose on the punching bag).

No one else can make me happy, but other people sure try to make me mad! She laughed, thinking of Kev, Abby and Marble.

But here's the thing, I choose a different ending to my story. I don't have to be mad all the time:
— Mad at Kev,
— Mad at mom and dad,
— Mad at Abby,
— Mad at Marble,
— Mad at myself.
I feel powerful when I'm mad, coz it's so intense, but then after, I feel drained and sad. And there's always damage control to be

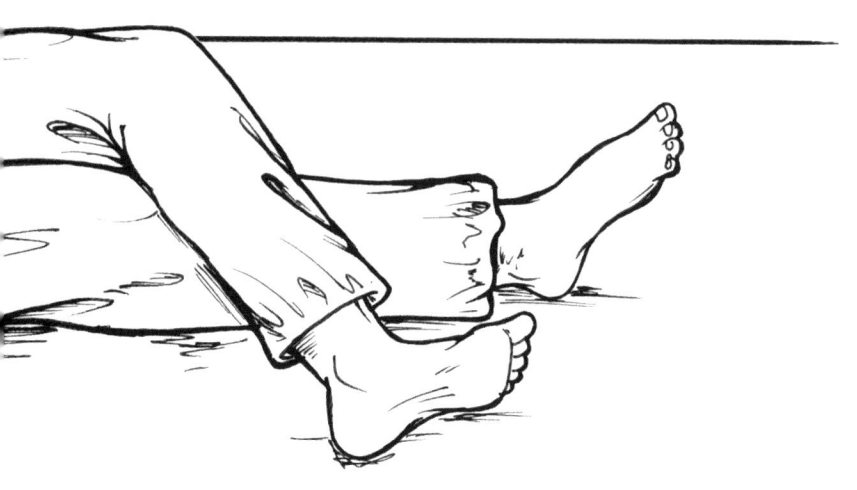

done. Being angry sucks! But I don't have to feel lousy all the time...

Other people may try to make me do or not do stuff, but they can't control the way I feel.

Only I can do that.

I choose how I react to things.

And now I've got all these tools to help me...

Zoey closed her eyes and thought of all the things she'd used to help her out of sticky situations in the barn, at school and at home...

BREATHE.

When I start to feel panicked, hurt, angry, or any other crappy emotion, I can just take some deep breaths. Everything slows down and doesn't seem like such a life and death situation — gives me time to let my mind catch up to my body and choose my reaction. In fact, when I breathe, things that were karazee become sorta... well... almost funny...

EXERCISE.

Remember when I was so angry, it hurt?

When I took my feelings out on the punching bag, I was releasing my pain in a positive way.

I turned pain into promise, inside me.

I went from feeling like crap to feeling awesome...

I can do that every time and it doesn't just have to be through sports.

It could be through lots of creative things — art, music, dancing, cooking...anything I love to do really.

WRITING.
Writing's cool...
It helped me sort out all that mumbo jumbo Ama was always talking about:
— Inner strength.
— People being like a mirror.
I was so confused at first, but then I wrote how I felt and what I was thinking. I started to see it more clearly...

CHOICE.
No matter what happens, I always have a choice.
Things really sucked a couple months back.
Everything was going wrong. I got into my first fight at school, ever! Even Marble got injured from that firecracker...
It coulda gotten a lot worse though. Being mad coulda just gone on forever.
But when I chose to stay calm and to forgive, everything got better — almost magically.
I may not be able to decide how people treat me, but I always decide how I'm gonna deal with it.
That makes me feel stronger inside already... like there's something inside me no one can take away...

All of a sudden, Zoey sat up, switched on her desk lamp and grabbed her journal from under her bed. With pen in hand, four words took shape on the page...

Breathe...
Exercise...
Write...
Choose...

She mulled the words over her tongue a few times...
Breathe starts with B. Exercise begins with E. Writing is W. And Choice is C. Hmm...interesting...
She wrote the letters by themselves on a fresh page...

B.E.W.C.

Sounds like 'puke' but with a 'B'. Cool... that's how I'll remember it.

BEWC your feelings and your anger goes away...

BEWC your feelings and you'll be better...

BEWC your feelings and it's all good...

Taking a deep breath, she tucked her journal safely under bed, sunk her head into her goose down pillow, pulled her comforter up to her chin and closed her eyes.

 BEWC. That feel's right to me. I can do that. That stuff'll make me stronger on the inside... Ama calls that inner strength... and you know what? It FEELS good.

I choose a different way... I don't wanna get angry all the time. Why???

Coz now I know that anger's not my power... LOVE is.

HEY KIDS

watch for

the next ZOEY LEE book...

- What do you think could happen in the next book?
- What adventures do you want Zoey to have?
- Who do you want to meet and get to know?

Submit your ideas here and enter to win a visit to your school by the author, L.M. Ling.

www.zoeyleebooks.com

Sign up and become part of the process of choosing chapter titles, illustrations and book titles, and edit the next book with the author. See your ideas in print!

Acknowledgements

For all the friends and family who have supported me along the way, including those who told me the book sucked!

Thank you for your honest feedback!

You pushed me to make it better.

For all the kids who came through the Jakarta International School (Indonesia) library and lent their ideas in the very early stages as Zoey was just taking shape. Thank you!

For class 3B (2010-11) at American School Doha (Qatar), who expanded the idea of the book, and helped create the Playbook and Teacher's Resource. You ROCK!

For all the kids in Jakarta, Doha, Canada, USA, and around the world who've added their idea fingerprints to this book. Thank you, thank you, thank you! You're AWESOME!

It was your enthusiasm that kept me going when I was feeling down and discouraged during the 5 years it took from original idea to publishing. You, yes you.

Many heads, hands and hearts have gone into the creation of this book.

You could even say it is a Co-Creation of ALL of us....

My deepest gratitude and appreciation for you all.

About the Author

This book was inspired by a little idea a friend dropped into my head when she emailed me and said "why don't you write a martial arts book for girls?"

That little, one sentence idea entered my mind like a seed, and it just wouldn't leave. Over the next 5 years it grew and grew (yeah, I watered and fed it...) until it became this book, the first of the Zoey Lee series!

That's right, there's more Zoey comin'!

When I started writing this story, I threw out my first draft because I thought it was lousy. I was so discouraged that I didn't write anything else for 6 months! But the pull of that little idea was too strong to resist. Gradually, I wrote more and more until I thought I had finished the book. I passed it to some friends who basically said "this needs a lot of work." So I went back to square one. I was pretty disheartened so I took a break from it for awhile to start writing short stories on a blog, teaching myself how to write.

I was also getting back into meditating after having 2 kids and found that all the ideas for the story came to me when I was quiet and still. When I could actually hear my own inner voice. (Not the voice that would tell me to eat a whole box of cookies...the other one:~) I read a bunch of children's books, watched the entire Star Wars series and soaked up stories of all kinds so I could learn how to tell them. For 2 years, ideas about the story of Zoey dropped into my head and I just collected them. Drop by drop, the story bucket filled up. And when the bucket was ready to overflow, I went away by myself for 10 days to eat, drink, live and breathe Zoey without any distractions, and wrote the entire book in 10 days.

We all have incredible stories in us that are waiting to come out. We all have dreams. What are yours?

It IS possible to overcome your fears and DO IT. Just start.

FOLLOW YOUR DREAMS!

* * *

L.M. Ling is a world soke cup karate champion, lawyer, and mother who's lived in 6 countries on 4 continents. She's been through a lot of 'dark tunnels' in life on her way here. Don't think it's all smooth sailin' on the path to your dreams, coz it isn't! But it sure is worth it :~). GO FOR IT!

Send me your thoughts on this book.
  What did you like?
    What didn't you like?
      How did the book affect you?

I'd love to hear from you!

Visit me at www.zoeyleebooks.com

Love TANK parenting

Let go of punishment, and create a peaceful and harmonious family with love.

Punishment is using fear to control your child. Is unquestioned obedience what you really want for your children? Is a relationship of authority and submission what you really want with your child?

Or do you want to trust them to listen to their own inner guidance?

When children misbehave, they need MORE love, not less love. Change the foundation of your relationship to one of <u>mutual understanding and respect</u>, maintaining <u>boundaries</u> and <u>natural consequences</u> of one's actions. Let go of control and let life teach them the lessons they are meant to learn. And let "DO YOU NEED A HUG?" become the most frequently asked question in your home.

This book is included with the course *Email from Aha!*

www.fear2love.com

want your parents to "get more love?"

transform FEAR & ANGER into LOVE
in everyday life

change from daily emotional explosions
to a peaceful and harmonious family

transforming...
www.fear2love.com